Annasheeva

Annasheeva

a novel

Virginia Young

Riverhaven Books

www.RiverhavenBooks.com

Annasheeva is a work of fiction. While some of the settings are actual, any similarity regarding names, characters, or incidents is entirely coincidental.

Published in the United States by Riverhaven Books, www.RiverhavenBooks.com

ISBN : 978-1-937588-54-0

Printed in the United States of America

Designed and Edited by Stephanie Lynn Blackman
Whitman, MA

With special thanks to my loyal readers
for your feedback and support.

Also by Virginia Young

Out of the Blue
A romance set in Massachusetts

The Birthday Gift
A romance set in Connecticut

Sleepless Tides
A romance set in Maine

Winter Waltz
A romance set in Vermont

By a Thread
A contemporary novel

Find Me
A collection of short stories and poetry

A Family of Strangers
A romantic suspense set in Canada and New Hampshire

I Call Your Name
A romantic suspense set on Martha's Vineyard

Nocturnal
A young adult novel

Where Seagulls Sleep
A romantic suspense set in Rhode Island

Chapter One

Each step she took in the moist sand became a subtle indentation, the salty sea flirting and swirling around her feet as the ocean swells retreated. The long, colorful skirt spiraled at her slim ankles as she moved: her eyes always in search of a pretty stone, a well-washed shell. At this time of day, she often had the beach to herself.

She bent gracefully to pick up a green-gray stone with flecks of silvery mica gleaming in the rising sun. She stood transfixed, the stone in her left palm, and looked straight ahead. The figure one-hundred feet away, walking toward her, was not familiar. She shivered for no known reason and pulled long strands of gray-blonde hair from her eyes. She stood there, statue still, until his slow but steady swagger caught up with her motionless stance.

"Hi," he said as he slowed and stopped next to her. "Nice morning, isn't it?"

Usually not hesitant to reply, she barely breathed as she acknowledged and agreed with an almost whispered, "Yes."

His gray eyes moved from her pretty face to her bare feet, then back to her blue eyes. He smiled. "I'm new here. Are you lucky enough to make this place your home? It's really beautiful."

"I live here, yes," she said, knowing that something had just occurred that would in some way alter her life.

He nodded then tucked his hands into jean pockets. "Nice," he said, and then he pulled one hand free and extended it toward her. "Shane Bellows."

She continued to look at him, shifted the sandals from her right hand to left after carefully balancing her shells and stones, then placed her hand briefly in his. "Annie," she said.

Neither of them moved; it was awkward. Finally, it was Shane who nodded, told her to enjoy her walk, then took a few steps away with a slight wave of his hand.

Annie swallowed and wondered what had just happened. In a matter of a few moments, she questioned why this man had a penetrating effect on her: friend, child, brother, nephew, lover? She could imagine him as any of those, close to her, except for one thing. At forty-nine, she suspected he was not more than thirty – far too young for her to entertain anything other than a casual thought.

"Annie," he called as she moved in the opposite direction. She stopped and, before she could turn around, he was there, before her. "Do you come here often? I was wondering if we could walk together sometime. It would be nice to have someone to talk to."

Annie could feel her heartbeat quicken. "I usually walk early in the morning and again early in the evening."

"Would it be okay for me to join you? Maybe not every time," he said. "I don't want to infringe on your space."

It was as if he had read her mind. Walking on the shore was Annie's reflective time, a time to soothe her mind and her feet. Tendons had been stretched to unreasonable measures dancing for the prestigious Katrina Ballet Company of New York. It had not occurred to her in her teens and twenties that in midlife she might suffer immense pain; continually forcing toes, arches, and heels into disagreeable positions hour after hour, day after day, year after year.

Annie brushed her windswept hair away from her face and squinted into the sun and his remarkable pewter grey eyes. "If we find ourselves here at the same time, we could walk together, yes."

Her voice was so low, Shane wasn't sure that she'd given her approval to the idea. He smiled slightly, revealing even white teeth behind his full lips.

Annie couldn't quite believe the immediate draw she felt to him. This was unsettling.

"Great," he said and then he turned to continue away from Annie. She twisted around to watch him stride away. With a slight limp on one side, his long legs took three-foot sections of damp sand at one time. Wondering if she could keep up with his pace, she turned again and began to walk slowly, this time closer to the surf, lifting her skirt to her knees as she enjoyed the cool energy of the sea on her ankles and calves. She raised her eyes from the shore to the sky, watching as brilliant sun made its entrance into day. *Shane. Shane*. Annie silently repeated his name as if it was a prayer, and still she did not know why. A heart-shaped stone in the shallow water caught her eye and she bent to pick it up. Then she spotted a tangerine-colored shell and scooped that up as well.

The sea, she thought, was filled with gifts to heal both body and soul. Standing straight, her eyes on the horizon, she thought about her years with Albert. The passionate conductor had been her mentor, her companion, and then her husband. Fifteen years her senior, she found him at first to be interesting and then to be caring and filled with tender charm. In her mind, Albert was above her in every way – he fascinated her with his European good looks and suave manner in which he detailed his life. They laughed often when she reminded him that she was his marionette. He was the maestro for the ballet company, directing the refined orchestra; she was the dancer to each essential beat. He had been her everything for more than half her life. Now he was gone.

It was impossible to think of Albert as still, his arms lifting toward the ornate opera house ceiling causing vibrant music to surround the stage, the audience. Surely the walls must have surrendered themselves to the depth and beauty of the pulsing sounds he ordered.

Annie walked for another ten minutes. She'd started at five-thirty; it was past seven. She reversed her steps and headed toward home, noting the scattered humans, some with their dogs, dotting the sandy shore.

She stopped at a small open market near town and purchased nectarines, cucumbers, and lettuce, freshly picked blueberries, and one stalk of bright green celery. She favored the scones and muffins but understood that she did not need added weight on her throbbing feet. With her purchases in a paper bag, Annie made her way through town to her cottage, nestled at the edge of a small pond with a cluster of pines on each side. She'd burned her bridges with New York. After Albert's illness and eventual death, she could not live where they had roamed the streets and made their home in his elegant brownstone. She sold the house then bought her tiny two-bedroom cottage on the southern shores of Massachusetts.

Once home, Annie placed the vegetables in her refrigerator and left the blueberries and nectarines on the kitchen's chestnut-topped island. She slipped into the shower to wash sand from her feet then returned to the kitchen and heated herself a cup of coffee. She stood looking out to the small pond and garden then sat down at her kitchen table.

Her thoughts went to Shane. Part of her wanted to avoid him while part of her wanted to ask him questions as she listened intently to the answers. He was a beautiful looking man, but there was more. He had a vulnerability to him, and yet he was confident and charming. Annie smiled and shook her head: *must not go there*.

When her eighteen year-old cat, who came with the cottage, wandered out to the kitchen, it was to remind Annie that cat food was in the cupboard and her dish was empty. Annie reached down to gently stroke the large, mostly white feline. With a touch of gray at the center of her head and covering most of one leg, she always made Annie think she'd forgotten her other sock.

"Okay, Daisy," Annie said as she spooned a can of food into the cat's dish, "there you are." Watching her for a moment, Annie took her cup of coffee to the living room and sat down, her slender feet up on the old trunk she'd arranged in front of her sofa.

Annie leaned back and closed her eyes, then opened them and followed the wooden beams at the ceiling, as if they were paths to her soul. She wondered who had built this little home, tucked back from the road. Even when sitting on her screened front porch, she was rarely noticed as people passed by. This was what she wanted, a quiet existence. She couldn't help but think of years earlier when life was anything but calm. Albert had not chosen to visit his family in Austria. He kept busy composing and performing, to the extent that Annie often felt abandoned. He did not speak of his home country unless asked, and when letters came from his mother, he read them and folded them away. Whatever he'd left behind in Europe, it was his choice. He'd been kind and generous with the love of his life, the elegant ballerina, Annasheeva.

Annie flexed her feet, turning her ankles in circles as had been suggested to her by a podiatrist in New York. "Keep your feet and legs moving, but gently; you've stressed them enough," he'd said.

She stood, carrying the now empty cup to the kitchen where Daisy sat cleaning her white whiskers. Annie stepped gracefully around the cat and then cut up two nectarines for her own breakfast. She decided she would read later out on the porch.

She had a system; there were four rooms in the cottage; each day Annie tidied one of them. This day, before settling down with a book, she would give the kitchen a proper washing. No employed help as she'd known in New York, no need. Albert had secured a dependable housekeeper long before he'd fashioned a life with his Annasheeva. Annie liked Mrs. May; there was no reason to change anything when she married and moved from a closet-sized apartment to the spacious eleven-room brownstone Albert had chosen years before.

Annie's blonde hair, pale blue eyes, and lithe form had enchanted him. Her fluid movements on stage appeared to deftly coincide with the penetrating music he'd directed. Notably, his work became softer, as if he'd composed it with her in mind.

His adoration of Annie was evident to everyone involved with each new project. Audiences were drawn to attend new productions simply to observe the magnificence of the pair working together. There was Albert with his entire being expressing every precise note; Annasheeva's body flowing and lifting weightlessly, almost like a fledgling learning to take wing. Aside from the engaging music and interpretation of dance, the two were cause for the audience to gasp with complete joy.

Her food consumed and the kitchen cleaned, Annie chose open windows and ocean breeze rather than central air. She preferred the quiet, the chirping of birds, the sound of life rather than a machine and home closed to the outdoors. She took her book and a glass of water to the porch, looked at the clock on the wall, and noted it was after two. She planned to read and later walk on the nearby shore while it was still bright.

Shane. Will Shane be there? Annie smiled at her girlish thoughts and before Daisy's tolerant stare she slapped herself gently on her left leg. Stop it, she told herself. *I may never see him again.*

With forty plus pages read, Annie rested her head on the back of the sofa and closed her eyes. She thought now and then of Washington Square Park, the bustling sea of humanity, some with their dogs, others feeding the tame squirrels. The park was near their home and her favored place to spend time. In her own little cottage, Annie felt a sense of taking care of herself, of living without schedules and appointments. The reality was that Albert was gone. Now she was willing to forfeit that vibrant city for a calm life. Without Albert by her side, Annie felt lessened. Somehow, the change had given her the resilience to carry on independently – she could well manage this casual mode of living.

Her novel left open on the trunk, Annie walked to the kitchen, thinking about what she would have for dinner and when she might head to the shore.

Neighbors watched her – each step graceful. They didn't know that painful arches contributed to movements natural for a former ballerina. They didn't know Annie's background – she was simply an obviously beautiful woman from New York, quiet about who and what she had been. Few people had won her confidence. Friends in New York had been shared acquaintances of Albert's. Other than creating and performing music, he liked to cook and to have people in for meals and good wine. Annie enjoyed the merriment and intelligent conversation, although between heavy rehearsals and Albert's choices for a lively existence, she did not find time to cultivate friendships with other women her age. And if she had, she might have met with resistance.

Annasheeva was the epitome of grace, on stage and in her life. She was serenely quiet and possessed an innate ability to move her slender form as if she had no bones, only cooperative muscles and pale, taught skin covering them. She drew attention in her casual walks, her hair loosened, flowing free in the gusts of wind around New York's towering structures. Dressed in jeans, boots, and a loose fitting jacket with a colorful scarf trailing her body, Annie enjoyed a fast-paced walk, unrecognized without her ballet costumes and tightly coiled hair. Purposely now, she allowed the mix of blonde and pale gray to cascade about her shoulders, seldom up in any form.

At seven, Annie placed a fresh can of food in Daisy's dish, told her she'd soon be home then slipped into a long, lime-green skirt and loose-fitting black shirt. She glanced in her hall mirror, pushed and pulled at her hair, then locked the house and left. She told herself with every step toward the sea that if Shane wasn't there, it would be for the best. It would be okay. But she also told herself, without meaning to, that she would be disappointed.

Nearing the shoreline, Annie slipped out of her

sandals and held them in her left hand. Carefully, balanced like a tight-rope walker, she made her way over the sizeable rocks to the sand. The tide was out, the beach dotted with families playing in the surf. She looked as far as she could for Shane. With a silent sigh, she looked out to the green-blue ocean and then began to walk. Near the jetty, she glanced up and saw him standing near a slice of rock more toward shore than surf. When he saw her, he stood and walked closer.

"Hi," he said with a nod, "I was hoping you'd be here."

Annie said nothing as she slowed her pace and he moved to place himself at her side. "I suppose I'm going to get my shoes wet, aren't I?"

Annie looked down at his sneakered feet. "I walk in the moist part of the sand, but I do like the shallow water as well."

Shane stopped, Annie waited a few feet ahead of him as he traded his foot gear for bare feet. He bent and rolled his jeans up two inches then stood and smiled. "I must look about three," he said.

Annie smiled. "*Everyone* on the beach looks three."

They walked on, side by side, as if they had been accustomed to one another for years. After several minutes of silence, except for the crashing waves and screeching gulls, Shane selected another large rock and asked Annie if she'd like to sit for a while.

"Sure," she replied softly.

Shane noticed the way she positioned herself on the rock with an athletic prowess one might expect from a gymnastic champion. He noted her pale eyes and her Cupid's bow lips.

"How long have you lived at Salt Hill Bay?" he asked looking at her and the shoulder-length hair that moved in the cool evening breeze. "Did you grow up here?"

Annie looked straight ahead, always intrigued by the horizon defining sea and sky. "I've been here for a couple of years."

Shane was surprised. She had the air of someone who had lived there forever. In fact, he couldn't imagine the place without her. It occurred to him that he felt roped in by this beautiful woman. He knew she was older – he didn't care. Annie was like no other woman he had ever known.

"I don't mean to pry," he said, "but where did you live before here?"

"New York City; and you?"

Shane dropped his sneakers to the sand and moved further back on the rock to line himself up with his companion.

"I finished four years in the service after I spent a year and a half in Afghanistan, then home. I grew up in Pennsylvania. I tried going back there a few months ago, stayed for a while working the farm with my dad, then decided to see the ocean, and here I am."

"Will you be going back there?"

Shane brushed sand off his jeans. "No. To visit, maybe, but as beautiful as the farm is, I just can't do it. It's heavy work, long hours. I took a little damage in the Army. My right side – hip, leg, and shoulder – kind of got in the way of enemy fire."

Annie looked at him. "That's terrible," she said. "Are you okay?"

Shane looked to the sea. "I will be. I just couldn't do the heavy work my dad expected of me. I felt like I was disappointing him. He didn't say that, but…it was awkward."

He remembered the look on his mother's face when

he told her he was leaving for parts unknown. She said little, but her dark blue eyes reflected the combination of tension and sorrow.

"Your family must have been sad to see you go again."

Shane turned to Annie. "I disappointed them both. I didn't want to tell them about the injuries. They knew I'd been hit, but I was hospitalized in Germany; I minimized the issue so they wouldn't worry."

Annie swallowed and said nothing for several minutes.

"What will you do? Are you thinking of staying here at Salt Hill?"

Shane smoothed back his dark blond hair. "I'm living on savings at the moment, but I know my way around a computer. I'm applying for a job where I can work at home at least part-time. That is, when I find a home." He smiled at Annie. "I'm staying at the Salt Hill Inn by the intersection, but that's not going to work for long. Apartments are hard to find in the tourist season. You don't happen to know of any, do you?"

She lightly bit her lower lip, "I'm sorry, no. I wish I did."

Shane shrugged his shoulder, the one closest to Annie. "I'll find something. Would you like to continue our walk?" Shane slid down off the rock and then turned to offer his hand to Annie. She took it and gracefully braced her legs and feet to connect with the sand. They released their hands once both were standing freely.

"Are you sure you're up to going further?" she asked.

Shane looked at her and, before he answered, his eyes scanned her alluring face. "Walking is good for me."

He took the first steps; Annie caught up with him as he turned to see if she was following. They walked along the damp shore without words. They had made a start to knowing one another and now it was the comfort of being with an agreeable companion in a generously beautiful setting.

After fifteen minutes, it was Annie who stopped and suggested they turn around.

"We have a good half mile back," she said, "and the tide will be chasing us further toward shore."

The wind caught her hair spilling it across her face. They laughed and then Annie gathered it together in one hand and held it until they were free of that particular gust. They looked at the lights on the street parallel to the shore – everything, the lanterns and small cafes, were aglow with invitations to the evening's darkening sky. This was Annie's favorite time of day, when windows were warmed by lights, seeming settled down, ready to welcome their inhabitants home.

Before the rocks to the road, Annie stopped and slipped her sandals back on. Shane followed suit. He offered his hand as they maneuvered the slight incline to the road and level land, then they both let go.

"Which direction for you?" he asked.

"To the left for about three blocks."

Shane nodded. "I'm about three blocks to the right, unless you'd like to have a drink someplace."

Annie's heart thumped with the thought. "Perhaps another time?" She simply was not prepared to spend more time with Shane. This was an unexpected friendship, and yet it was filled with a gentle sweetness she had not known with another man. They parted with the promise of a morning walk.

Annie turned to make her way to the cottage and thought about Albert. He was thirty-eight to her twenty-three years when they married. Annie accepted Albert's suggestions for where they went for dinner and who they invited to their home. Nothing he did was objectionable, but it did leave her out of decisions.

Shane turned around to watch her walk away, her lime skirt lifting just above slim ankles as she moved. He smiled, tucked his hands into his jean pockets, and walked toward his hotel.

Annie entered her cottage through the front porch. She stepped inside and leaned against the door, her eyes closed. *What am I getting into?* She opened her eyes and turned on the two lights in the living room, Daisy meeting her with a soft mew. Annie scooped the large cat up into her arms and told her how lovely she was, then she put the squirming feline down as she kicked off her sandals and enjoyed the cool floor against her bare feet.

It would be another evening alone. She could have accepted Shane's offer for a drink, but what were the intentions of this new friendship? She concluded that it would be best to stick to the walks on the beach, the light conversation. A relationship such as this could become entangled – it had nowhere to go.

Annie mixed a pitcher of lemonade, dropped three ice cubes into a glass, then poured herself an ample serving. She checked for locked doors, dimmed several lights, then took a few sips of her drink before changing into cotton pajama bottoms and a loose fitting t-shirt. She watched TV and read, a huge change from what she had grown accustomed to in New York. Each page she read refused to distract her from thinking about the good-looking young man new to her life. TV was not interesting, but it was background noise, like something alive in the house other than Daisy and herself.

Thinking that a person could surround oneself with

people and places, or making a move as she had, Annie learned that it was impossible to escape old memories and simple loneliness. A handful of years had not mended the torn existence she had thought would endure forever.

Tomorrow, she thought, I will work in the garden. I will walk on the beach and then I will weed through the Verbena and Russian Sage. After that, I will tackle my bedroom closet.

Her life was about keeping orderly and staying independently well. She thought about her childhood and what was left of her family. Albert had immigrated to America from Austria – Shane had given up on Pennsylvania, and she had long ago left the lush Connecticut hills.

Chapter Two

Morning filtered bright light through screens and lace to Annie's closed eyes. She squinted as she realized that a ten-pound cat was draped across her middle and the usually orderly sheets were askew on the double bed.

Gently, Annie pet and moved Daisy. Slipping bare feet to the floor, she apologized to the lethargic feline and asked, "Are you hungry?" Daisy blinked lazily and swished her tail as a non-committal response. Annie smiled, but she knew that age was catching up to her sweet companion.

In the kitchen, Annie made coffee before opening her back door to the garden. Hummingbirds danced in midair at pale purple blooms, and butterflies moved gracefully from wild roses to the yellow Japonica bush. There was nothing like this at her home in New York. Wildlife and flowers were found in the park at Washington Square where she and Albert had walked most evenings. Now Annie felt grateful to the elderly couple who had sold their home to her – they had invested time and money to create and keep the back garden filled with beauty and generous supplies of nectar.

With black coffee consumed on her front porch, Annie left Daisy with a fresh can of food and water. Changing into an ankle-length dress in shades of blue, she moved her feet into sandals, grabbed a small basket for her beach finds, and made her way to the shore. Each step she took was accompanied by thoughts of Shane – would he be there? Half of her hoped he would not. Half of her felt a longing to see him again, if even for a few moments. She had not known this yearning for a connection to any other human being. A young and active dancer, she had no time for anything other than her creative life, and then there was Albert. Albert had selected Annie for his elegant compositions – he'd observed her interpretation of his work and then he fell in love with her. Being adored by her audience was not the same as being adored by a sophisticated man with a vibrant city in awe of his abilities.

Stepping carefully over boulders to the sand, she did not see that Shane was just a few feet away. She bent slightly to take the sandals from her feet and, when she stood, he was there like a magical ghost.

"Good morning," he said with his hand extended to help her navigate the smaller stones before reaching silky sand.

Tentatively, she took his hand and then found her voice. "Good morning."

She noticed that he had rolled his jeans up above his ankles and his shoes were in his right hand. They began to walk as if there had been a plan, each of them with their eyes on the incoming tide.

After fifteen minutes of walking, their feet leaving molded forms in the damp sand, they arrived at the rock where they had rested the evening before.

"Shall we?" he asked as he nodded toward the smooth boulder.

This was new to Annie; she had always walked the beach alone then turned and walk back toward town and her home. She moved with him to the rock and, like a feather, hoisted herself up.

Shane smiled. "You look like a mermaid sitting there with that long dress over your legs."

Annie smiled but she could feel heat rush to her face and hoped it hadn't been evident to him. He used his arms to move up near to her, an obvious struggle. She said nothing of his awkward moves and neither did he.

"Have you had any luck finding an apartment?" she asked.

Shane shook his head. "No, still looking. I did get a job though, the one I told you about. I'll be able to work at home."

Annie felt a sudden rush as she wondered what this would mean to their walks. "That's wonderful."

"Yeah, I'm really glad about this. I start in two weeks."

They were both quiet, eyes to the sea. Annie had questions, but she decided to keep them to herself.

"I'll be able to walk with you most of the time," he said, answering her most significant concern. "In fact, I think it will be the best thing for me, getting up and starting early. Then in the evenings, it will be nice to unwind with another stroll on the beach."

Annie said nothing, but her heart pranced with the idea that she would have a companion to walk with. She would keep their relationship casual. He was young and interesting, and that was as far as she would allow their friendship to evolve.

Shane studied her. "Can I ask you a question?"

Annie looked at him and shrugged slightly. "I suppose so."

"Before you came to Salt Hill, you lived in New York City. What did you do there?"

Annie looked down at her bare toes and then to the sea. "I was a dancer."

Shane laughed. "No wonder you move like you do. You almost look like you're on strings, you know, like a puppet."

Annie's heart picked up extra beats as she thought about the analogy of her private joke with Albert, that she was his marionette, he her master.

"What kind of dancing?"

Startled by the question in the middle of her thoughts, Annie looked at Shane. "Ballet," she stammered.

Shane looked at her, the softness of her expression, her shoulder length hair gently moving with the morning breeze. "Ballet," he repeated, and then they were quiet as they slid off the boulder and onto the sand to complete their walk. Annie stooped to examine a stone and then a shell which she placed in her basket.

"What do you do with these treasures?" he asked.

Annie tucked strands of hair behind her left ear. "I put them in my garden. They look nice there."

Although she did not see him smile, his silence gave her the assurance that he approved. With their walk completed, Shane invited her to have coffee with him. Once again, she felt a chill as she gave him a reason why she could not.

He looked at her for several moments while she slipped sandals on her feet. Everything about her, the way she looked, the way she moved, the way she spoke, seemed unfamiliarly perfect.

Annie looked up at his eyes and unconsciously smiled.

"What?" he asked, returning the smile. "Did a seagull get me?" He ran a hand over his thick hair.

Annie laughed. "No. But they say it's good luck."

"Good luck for who?" he asked with a grin. "If it happens just once, I'll take to wearing a cap. Has it ever happened to you?"

"No, the gulls have been very well-behaved toward me."

Shane nodded. He could imagine that everyone would be well-behaved with Annie. He looked toward the sea again and then back at his companion's serenely beautiful face. "Are you sure about that coffee? My treat."

Annie scuffed her feet and adjusted the basket in her hands. "Thank you. I really can't." And that was true; Annie could not allow herself to slide into a relationship so unimaginable. He was handsome, charmingly shy at times, and she knew that Shane Bellows could become too significant in her life.

Moments later, safely inside her cottage, Annie took a deep breath. As usual, she rinsed the sand from her feet, the cool water from the shower flowing from her ankles to toes. After a cup of coffee, she straightened her bedroom closet and then worked in the garden. Later, with Daisy next to her on the sofa, she sat with her book and a cucumber and butter sandwich, intent on finishing that novel so that she might start another.

Without having read the last few pages, Annie felt restless and walked to her kitchen window. So much of her was out there in that garden; a little statue of a ballerina holding out her hand, a gift long ago from Albert. There was enough indentation in that palm to hold a small amount of sunflower hearts. Annie smiled watching the variety of birds eating from that dainty hand, an offering for bringing her garden to life.

She thought back to walking in the park at Washington Square. That space had been her daily ritual, a connection to nature. She missed it: the lovely old trees, the squirrels scampering about, the walkways lined with inviting benches. But this little garden, one which Albert would have heartily laughed at for its diminutive size, was more of Annie than any other space.

She turned from the window, her hands resting on the counter behind her. She looked around the small, white room. Touches of red here and there brought the remembered spirit of the city, memories she did not want to lose. That part of her was past, impossible to navigate without Albert. Yet there, in that small cottage by the sea, resolve was found. Annie had made each day a composition of work and relaxation. She had not encouraged friendships but remained sociable with people in town. No one there knew she had performed for kings or that she saw her face and figure on billboards high up in Times Square. None of that mattered ever. Had it not been for Albert finding and convincing her to dance, she might have left it all behind for a more simple life. It had been Albert, captivated with her grace and capturing her heart, who had persuaded her that she must stay – she must dance. Somehow, it was owed.

Annie stepped away from the sink and moved her right foot as if she might make the small kitchen floor her stage. And then she stopped. Her ankle revolted in pain; it was not worth it to renew the feeling of once again displaying her art, and, if she did, for whom? She wondered if she would enjoy the graceful movements or if she would further torment her body. Annie stepped back, took one more glance at the garden, then walked into her living room.

On the trunk she kept two large albums filled with programs and pictures from her days on stage. Sitting on the sofa, she lifted one album, looked at its worn cover, then placed it back. She hadn't looked at those pages since before Albert's death; she wasn't ready. It had occurred to her that they might be best kept on the shelf of her bedroom closet. Here, before her, they were a reminder of all she had lost and the emptiness she sought to fill with simplicity.

Annie gently rubbed her eyes and questioned her existence. She had money. There was no need to seek work. She had thought of volunteering, but to do what? She had inquired at the local hospital where she'd found people old enough to be her parents standing around chatting, occasionally guiding a visitor to the elevators or directing them to a particular level. There seemed to be more help than required, not something Annie would feel benefitted anyone. The thought of teaching children the art of ballet had come to mind, and that was still a possibility. Adjusting to life on her own was taking more time than Annie had imagined. Albert had been consuming. Dance had been what she did. Now, who was she? Filling her hours with keeping her space orderly and reading, walking the shorelines and weaving in and out of the shops in town was hardly enough to satisfy her soul.

Shane was adding an ingredient she had not thought to miss. He was interesting and companionable, and unlike others she'd met in this new environment, he had managed to insert himself into her life. She had not known how lonely she was until she met him.

Annie found herself watching the clock, waiting and wishing the day away until she would walk the shore at seven and, hopefully, see Shane. Noting the remnants of gardening on her dress, Annie decided to freshen up and change her outfit.

At her closet, she moved hangers across the metal bar

emitting slight screeching sounds. A blue dress was dismissed. A tan jersey and rust colored skirt were moved aside. She selected a dusty rose skirt and a fitted black shirt; the dark fabric against her pale hair a magical contrast. She smiled at her own vanity in making an effort to appear pleasing. It had been many years since she'd put this much interest and energy into dressing to please. It had once been a matter of costumes and comfortable attire at home. Albert had told her often that she would look wonderful in a brown paper bag. Along with his wife's mystical beauty and talent for dance, Albert knew the heart and soul of her; there wasn't anything he would deny her and yet she asked for nothing.

Slipping her feet into sandals, the key to the house in her skirt pocket, Annie gave Daisy a pat and a promise to be back soon.

He saw her making her way toward the beach and, while he might have moved forward to meet her, he instead stood and took in her graceful steps. He studied the way she moved her arms to balance herself on the rocks, the way the gentle breeze lifted her light hair and whisked it across the dark shirt. Everything about her was perfection.

On the sand, she looked up and saw him about thirty steps away. He smiled at her and she felt her heart constrict. She stopped momentarily and then proceeded toward Shane, emerging as though she had confidence in greeting him, which she did not.

"Hi," he said, hands tucked into his jeans.

"Hi," she returned.

They fell into even steps toward the water. A few feet from the rolling surf lapping against the damp shore, Annie hesitated and Shane stopped.

"Time for the shoes to come off?"

"Yes," she said. As she bent to take her sandals into her hands, she lost her balance for just a moment and Shane reached for her arm. The warmth of his hand on her elbow made Annie shiver.

Once she was steadied and with his own shoes in hand, he slowly, regretfully let go of her. They walked, their feet in the cool water.

"I love the ocean," he said. "Living in Pennsylvania and serving in the Middle East didn't provide much of an opportunity to enjoy the sea."

Annie's eyes were fastened to the ocean's swell, the continuing force so beautifully, constantly moving. As stunning as the Connecticut hills were, and as vibrant as New York City was, life by the sea was not only soothingly beautiful, it was a confirmation of life going on through storm and tranquil times.

"When you first came here, did you know you'd stay?"

Annie looked down at her feet and then back up at the sea. "Not really. I came for a weekend, just a getaway, but I knew when I was leaving to return to New York that I'd be coming back. Salt Hill was what I needed."

"Do you still feel the same? Has this been all you hoped for?"

Annie brushed the hair from her eyes and held it back briefly in place. "Yes."

They walked in silence for several minutes then came to their rock.

"Shall we?" he asked, beckoning toward the smooth boulder.

Not accustomed to stopping during her walks, Annie understood that Shane was recovering. He was well built but noticeably thin. Without a word, she walked toward the rock, shifted her body up to sit, then moved to accommodate Shane.

After a few quiet moments, Shane looked at her with a teasing smile. "Are you ever going to have a drink with me? You know, if you don't drink, that's okay. We can have a ginger ale, coffee, whatever you'd like. I'm a beer guy basically, but I can live without it."

Annie took a deep breath. "I like a glass of wine once in a while, but since living here I haven't had it. My husband knew wines. I never did. I trusted that when he poured us a glass with dinner, it would be good."

Shane looked at her eyes then traveled from her face to bare toes. When he looked back at her face he asked again, "So, will you have a drink with me?"

Annie smoothed her skirt and slid forward to the sand. "Maybe sometime," she said.

"Tonight?"

Annie reached the ground, her shoes in hand. "Not tonight."

Shane moved his long legs from the rock to the sand without question. They walked further away from town and then reversed their direction as the sun began to set.

Where Annie faultlessly made her way over the rocks to the sidewalk, they halted long enough to look at one another. Shane smiled as he noted Annie's tentative expression, as if he knew not to ask again about having a drink. He would think about how to find more time with her, but maybe a new tactic would be in order.

"So, who do you have waiting for you when you go home?" he asked.

Annie slipped her sandals onto her feet then stood straight. "My cat, Daisy."

Shane smiled. "Daisy - sounds good. I had a dog when I was a kid. Maybe I'll visit the local pound and get another one when I get settled."

Annie studied his face for a few moments longer than she had intended. "That's a good idea; give a dog in need a home."

She started to move away from him, hoping that he would not make the offer for a drink again. She was running out of excuses.

"Okay, then I guess I'll see you in the morning." Before she could respond, Shane gave her a little wave and turned to walk away.

Annie watched him for a moment before she backed up a few steps and then turned toward home. He had not mentioned a drink. That was comfortable, but now she wondered why. Don't give up on me, she thought, and then she silently scolded herself for wanting him to plead for the very thing she was avoiding. Relationships began, had their life, and ended. She'd had enough of endings, yet Shane had revived her interest in making a contact. If she kept him at arm's length, if she compelled herself to think of him as a friend and nothing more, perhaps she would consent to him in her life in some capacity.

Shane turned around in time to see her turn a corner and vanish from sight. She made him want more of her. Annie was timeless. Her blended gray and blonde hair was subtle, but evident. He didn't care – she was a magnetic combination of grace, intelligence, sweetness, and beauty. He was thirty-two – he guessed her to be near forty.

Chapter Three

Over the next few days, Salt Hill Bay became the victim of a powerful storm, closing beaches to all but unwavering seagulls flying at a slant, slicing through persistent winds.

Annie stood at her kitchen window, watching as her garden tolerated swaying stems, supported and teased by neighboring plants. Staked Cherry tomatoes stoically stood next to delicate Verbena, striking in its multicolor array of peach, yellow, and white. She thought about Shane, closed in a room without his own furniture and familiar things. What did he do on a day such as this? She pictured him making his way in the rain to a coffee shop or to a restaurant for dinner. At least, she thought, home was inviting and filled with her needs.

Annie went about her chores, sometimes spending just minutes to straighten or dust a room before settling down to TV or a book. She found herself feeling restless without her walks and distracted by wondering what Shane was doing. He'd made an impact. Reluctantly, she admitted that she missed him.

Daisy joined her as Annie sat with a book upside down on her lap. She moved the book to make room for the feline and then she hugged her close. "You and me, Daisy," she whispered into the cat's ear. It had been the two of them since she'd bought the cottage. Daisy's companionship had been enough, a time without stress or wishful thoughts. Now there was Shane Bellows.

On the third day of unrelenting rain, Annie pulled a light waist-length jacket over a long cotton dress. With a red umbrella, keys, and her wallet, she went out for a walk through town.

He watched her move at a fast pace, her eyes toward the irregular sidewalks, her hair blowing with the Atlantic gusts. She was a picture in that lavender dress with the brilliant red umbrella, looking much like a colorful cloud. She lowered and closed it into a narrow cone, then slipped into a bakery cafe.

Annie brushed the rain from the lower part of her dress and waited in line to order a coffee and blueberry muffin.

"Hey," he said as he came up behind her, "that better not be the last blueberry muffin you just ordered."

Annie turned and found herself inches from Shane. She smiled, or at least she thought she did, and then she felt suddenly weak. "I'll share if it is."

Shane smiled. "I'm teasing. But will you sit with me? I'll grab something and we can share a table and some thoughts."

Annie nodded then paid for her food. In a corner, she found a table that had just been vacated. She took napkins from a nearby counter and sat down, pulling the paper from the muffin's sides. Within moments, Shane was sitting next to her with coffee and a chunk of crumb-top coffee cake.

"That looks good," she said.

"Would you like to share it?"

Annie smiled. "No, thank you. Were the blueberry muffins gone?"

Shane returned her smile. "No, really, I was teasing

you. I like this cake."

They sipped their coffee in silence until Shane spoke. "I've missed you."

Annie could feel the traitorous flush. "The rain is a bit forbidding."

"And yet you're here."

Annie swallowed a few more sips of coffee then broke off a piece of muffin. "I felt the need to get out. Weather can be confining. I seldom walk the shores in cold and snow, but I meander through town. There are always friendly faces and pretty things to look at in store windows."

Shane was quiet as he looked at the perfection of her face. Tiny lines had taken their place at the corners of her eyes and he found himself wanting to kiss that soft tissue, to stroke her smooth cheek, to taste the bare lips. No make-up and, still, she was beautiful.

"I actually thought about asking you out for dinner," he said. "However, I realized I didn't even know your last name to look up your number."

Annie felt the flush once more.

Shane swallowed a piece of cake then looked at her as he wiped away crumbs from his mouth. He tilted his head and moved inches closer to her. "Any chance I could get your number? And what about dinner this evening?"

Annie felt her throat constrict. Since Albert, there had been no one.

He pushed a paper napkin toward her with a pen. She looked at it, brushed muffin crumbs from her fingers, then jotted down her telephone number and the complicated spelling of her last name.

Shane looked at what she had written. "Wow, that's a challenge to pronounce," he said with a smile.

"My husband was Austrian."

They were quiet for a few minutes as they ate their food and drank coffee. When Shane had finished the last of his cake, he pushed the small plate aside and asked, "So, will you have dinner with me tonight?"

Annie hesitated as she looked outside through a small window by their table. "Well, it's raining."

Shane laughed. "I have a car. I can pick you up. That is, if you tell me where you live."

Now her hesitation became more noticeable.

"Annie, it's just dinner. I thought it would be nice to have some company."

Annie forced a little smile and squirmed in her chair. When she found the bravado to look at him, she also found her voice. "Shane, I'm not so sure about this. Have you met other people in town? I mean, I enjoy our walks at the beach, but we have this, this age difference. Wouldn't you be more comfortable with people your own age?"

Shane had a crooked little grin on his lips as he looked at her. "Annie, who cares about the age thing? I don't."

Annie silently sighed. "Shane, I'm sure that I'm old enough to be your mother."

"I doubt that."

Annie looked around at people sitting together, having coffee and a sweet. She looked at Shane. "I'm sure that biologically I'm old enough to be your mother."

Shane sat back in his chair, his eyes fastened to her face. "I find that hard to believe, I really do. But what do I care how old you are? I don't care at all. Now, will you have dinner with me tonight?"

Annie folded her napkin next to her plate and stared at him. "Let's wait."

"For?"

29

"Better weather, a little more of us knowing one another, I don't know."

Shane huffed as he leaned forward in his chair and then sat up straight. "Please, don't make a wounded soldier beg."

Annie smiled. Her blue eyes twinkled and made her seem more youthful than he had guessed.

"I'm not giving up," he added with a serious expression.

Annie looked down at her empty cup and then back at Shane. "Some night, after we've walked the beach, I'll show you where I live. I'll make you dinner. I'm not a great cook, but I survive." She smiled and hoped that invitation would appease him.

"I'd like that," he accepted, "but I'm going nuts in my hotel room with this rain. I was really hoping you'd consent to dinner tonight."

Annie took a deep breath. "Okay. You win. I'm at Nineteen North Street, the cottage with a little fence and front porch."

"Six, seven?" he asked.

"Let's do seven," she said as she stood. "Where are we going? I'd like to wear something appropriate."

"What's good? You must have a favorite place."

Annie shook her head from side to side. "I haven't been to a restaurant since I moved here. I come here for coffee and muffins. That's it."

Shane looked at her as though he found her statement hard to believe. "Well then, I'll ask at the hotel where the locals like to dine. Let's be casual tonight, no ball gowns and black ties."

Annie smiled as she gathered her umbrella, keys, and wallet together. "Seven," she said, and then she cleared her side of the table, put her trash in the bin, and left the cafe.

Her walk home was swift and anxious. How had she let Shane talk her into dinner? And what was she thinking to tell him that she would have him over for a meal some night after their walk? He was persuasive, charming, and effective at winning his way.

Inside her cottage, Annie left her damp umbrella to dry on the porch as she made her way inside where Daisy sat waiting like an old maiden aunt. Depositing her keys and wallet on the kitchen table, Annie walked to her closet and studied her selection of clothes. She chose a black ankle-length skirt and a pale pink blouse for her evening with Shane. Even as she thought the words, 'evening with Shane,' she could not believe she had given in. She shivered, fed Daisy, then took a warm shower. This is not a date, she told herself; this is not a date.

With her hair still wet, she slipped a long, belted robe over her body and went out to sit on her porch. Daisy followed and perched herself among plants in the corner of the room where she could watch the birds. Annie closed her eyes and appealed to her inner self to explain why this evening was happening. How had she fallen into going out with Shane? The relationship had to be completely platonic. She would make certain that conversation as well as emotions were kept at a distance. They could be friends, nothing more.

With a nervous energy, Annie glanced at the clock in her kitchen. It was after four; she had three hours to compose herself before Shane would arrive. She brushed her hair, twisting it up on top of her head, then let it fall loose to her shoulders. She held the pink blouse to her skin and thought it might be washing her out – it didn't matter. This was going to be a meal with a friend, plain and simple. Shane, she thought, could be my son, my nephew. *I'll go out with him in that mode. I'll be his aunt. We'll talk; we'll have a nice time.* Adrenalin rushed.

At five minutes past seven, a sensible looking black car pulled up in front of Annie's house. The rain had stopped. She shooed Daisy back, locked the door, and met Shane as he was walking up the pathway.

"You look beautiful," he said, opening the car door for her.

Annie slid into the seat as he closed the door and went to take his place behind the wheel.

"I heard about a restaurant down on the main road," he said. "It's called The Sandbar. I was told it's casual and has good food."

"That sounds perfect," Annie said, concealing her shallow breaths.

Shane stole glances at Annie's profile. He could sense her nervous demeanor and her concentration on the road straight ahead. Within minutes they were pulling into the restaurant parking lot. She started to open her door when Shane opened it for her and extended his hand to help her out of the car. Once she was standing, she thanked him as their hands dropped away to their sides. Walking in and being seated, Annie made sure that she remembered what this was, an evening with a nephew.

Shane looked at her slender form and gleaming hair. Still without make-up, no one would have guessed that she was more than in her mid-thirties.

They were seated at a table with an ocean view as a candle gleamed in an amber-toned glass. It was a romantic setting, but, again, Annie reminded herself of who she was and what they were.

Their evening conversation was consciously kept unintended, gracefully non-exploratory. Shane understood that she had been the reluctant one. He made certain that he would ask no questions; Annie was his guest and there was no reason to put her ill at ease. They mentioned the weather, the promising sunset, the good food. He sampled a small piece of her clam cakes; she accepted a bite-sized portion of his Cajun coleslaw. Relaxation – no stress.

When the evening ended, Shane pulled up to Annie's front door, put his car in park, and looked at her. It was her move; that was clear. She thanked him for a wonderful meal and good company then reached for the handle of her door. He started to get out, realizing that this was the night's end.

"Don't get out, I'm fine." She'd noticed his walk into the restaurant as she had a few times at the beach. He'd not been explicit about his injuries in Afghanistan, but she suspected he had a measure of pain in at least one leg. "Thank you again," she said and then she turned toward the cottage.

"Hey," he shouted, "are we walking the beach tomorrow since the rain has stopped?"

Annie nodded. "I'll see you there."

Inside, she went over every detail of the evening, hoping she had said or done nothing to lead him on. He was young and sweet and, as much as she wanted him to find someone his own age, she knew that he would be missed. Annie reminded herself that she had managed to survive Albert's passing. It would not be easy, but losing Shane would happen – it had to.

Chapter Four

Weeks blended into months, with autumn arriving in vibrant gold and layers of crimson. Annie and Shane didn't miss a single morning or evening walk on the shores of Salt Hill Bay. Annie walked slower than she had before meeting Shane – she allowed him to set the pace, noting the pain each step might bring. His gentle words regarding his family impressed her. His views on war and the people of Afghanistan were logical and tender – Annie wondered if he had always held such empathy for human plight.

"Do you talk to your parents often?" she asked as they sat on their rock at the sea.

Shane's eyes were on the ocean, the evening sun was setting earlier now. "I call home about once a week. I talk to Mom usually; sometimes Dad picks up the phone, or my kid sister."

"They must miss you."

Shane kept his eyes to the sea. "They're pretty used to me being gone."

He hesitated and then continued. "After college, I tried going back to Pennsylvania. My dad didn't get that I wanted to do computer work – there was nothing near home for me to do, except farming. It was at that point that I joined the Army and found myself in the middle of a massive conflict." He looked at Annie and smiled. "It was okay, good life experience seeing how the rest of the world manages."

Annie took a deep breath and asked what she had been hesitant to address. "How bad were your injuries?"

Shane looked down and then back toward the sea. "They kind of chopped me up. Broken ribs, punctured lung, shattered hip and thigh bones. Duct tape and glue," he said with a smile as his eyes scanned her lovely face.

"Are you in pain?"

"Sometimes."

Annie swallowed back tears and looked to the unceasing waves. "Does the walking help?"

Shane looked at Annie. "It does when I'm with you."

Annie could feel the flush to her cheeks again – she didn't know what to say to that remark and said nothing. Walking with Shane had been an unexpected joy as she'd managed to keep the relationship casual. Her offer to have him over for dinner stayed in her thoughts. A promise made with sincerity, the thought of him in her home was compelling.

"Are we ready to go on?" he asked.

Annie slid off the rock, her bare feet displacing the moist sand. She smoothed her skirt and moved to place herself at Shane's side as he took a lengthy step. As if their thoughts mingled without effort, they walked in silence, each of them watching the rolling waves and graceful movements of the gulls. At one point, Shane bent to retrieve a shell for Annie. She noticed that when he stood, he closed his eyes for a moment and grimaced. She said nothing but knew that he was in pain.

"Maybe we should turn back," she said.

"Getting tired?"

Annie came to a stand-still. "A little."

They reversed their walk and slowed their pace.

"Any interest in sharing a pizza when we get back?" he asked.

"Didn't you eat?" she said with surprise in her question.

Shane shook his head. "No, I wasn't hungry, but I could use something."

Annie was quiet. *Now what?*

"Do you like corn chowder?" she asked.

"Haven't had any in years but, yes, I like it a lot."

Annie wondered how she'd cornered herself, but she continued. "I made some today, that's what I had for supper. Would you like some?"

Shane looked at her as they walked, a slight smile on his lips. "Is this an invitation to your house?"

Annie nodded. "Yes, it is."

"I accept."

They walked in stillness, their eyes toward the sea, as if it might change before them. Annie felt a knot in her chest that she was bringing this young man home with her. She felt determined to keep things casual, to act as if he were nothing more than a friend. And yet within her there was a craving to hold him close, despite being still uncertain how she saw him in her life. Her only certainty was how terrible it would be to lose him.

Shane walked with a steady gait, his hands tucked into jacket pockets. For split seconds he would steal glances at Annie's feet and then raise his gray eyes to the sea. This was the most beautiful woman he had ever known: physically and emotionally. His heart pounded with the idea of going to her home, seeing how she surrounded herself with life when she was not on the beach.

Annie moved in sync with Shane and wondered if he was as apprehensive as she about this invitation. She went over in her mind how she would entertain him.

Would she suggest he wash up while she heated the chowder? No, that was too much like being his mother. Would she suggest he sit in a favorite chair for comfort? No, she decided he should sit wherever he chose. She found the pace of her heart quickening. She'd thought about having him to her home before; the time had come.

Where shore met stones then sidewalk, Annie slipped her shoes back on her feet. Shane had placed his sneakers back on after time at their rock. He watched her, tempted to steady her by holding onto her arm. He pulled his hand away and stuffed it back in his pocket as they moved toward her home.

"Do you think Daisy will welcome me?" he asked with a smile to break their awkward silence.

Annie smiled as she watched her steps. "She'll probably be glad for another lap."

The walk to Annie's cottage took just another few minutes and was made without conversation. At the front door, Annie walked into her porch and unlocked the door to her living room. Shane looked around at the myriad of pastels: shades of pale green, lemonade yellow, and white. The only brilliant colors were stacked on white shelving, books of every shape and size. The place was warm, a reflection of her.

Daisy walked toward them and stopped in her tracks as she eyed Shane. He bent slightly and spoke to her. She stood motionless for a few moments then walked over to sniff his hands.

"Oh, so glad she didn't bite," Annie said with a straight face.

Shane stood up and looked at Annie.

"Just kidding," she laughed,

Shane relaxed and shrugged off his denim jacket, leaving it across a wicker rocking chair.

"Make yourself comfortable," Annie invited. "I'll just be a few minutes heating the chowder."

"Okay if I wash up?" he asked.

"Of course, first door on the right down this hall." She indicated that he should go to the left and then she turned toward the kitchen, her breath held with the first guest to her home. In New York, Annie had left the guests and food to Albert. Now she was on her own.

As she used a copper ladle to serve the chowder, Shane sat down at the small table in the kitchen. Annie placed two rolls and butter before him along with a cloth napkin. As if feeding a lion, she backed away and watched as he tasted the chowder.

"This is delicious. Thank you."

Annie asked what he'd prefer to drink. He chose water. She placed a glass of the clear liquid before him then poured herself a cup of coffee and sat down across from him.

She watched his left hand tremble slightly as he buttered a roll and took a bite. There was so much she didn't know about him, and yet she knew everything.

When his meal was finished, he looked at her. "This has been a treat. I can see why you don't go out to eat a lot. You're a good cook."

Annie smiled. "Not really. I can make a few things, enough to keep me satisfied."

Shane looked at the way she held her cup, with both hands.

"You don't go out for food much?"

Annie placed her cup down on the table. "Not much, no; for coffee, but not for a meal."

"Why not?"

Almost as soon as he'd asked the question, Shane knew the answer. It was awkward, no fun to go out for a meal alone.

Annie shrugged her slim shoulders as she watched him finish the last of his chowder then asked, "Would you like coffee?"

"I'd love it."

She poured coffee into a mug. He told her he took it black and then she invited him into the living room. She noticed that he was slow getting up from the chair at the kitchen table, carefully bracing himself.

In the living room, she hesitated before advising him to sit in the most comfortable of her chairs. Annie sat down on the sofa across from him. "Would you like TV on?"

Shane sipped his coffee and then placed the mug on a nearby table. "No, unless there's something you'd like to watch."

"There's nothing," she said as she moved her hair away from the collar of her blouse.

"I like your house. It's warm and inviting. I can see why you settled here."

Annie looked around and then back at Shane. "It's small, easy to take care of. I don't need a lot of space."

Shane shifted his position a bit, as if his hip might be bothering him. "Was your home in New York more spacious?"

Annie nodded. "Yes, my husband owned the house for years before we married."

Shane studied her face, always fascinated with her translucent beauty. "How old were you when you began to dance?"

"I took lessons in Connecticut when I was barely five. By the time I was eight, I was dancing in New York under the guidance of a female director my aunt knew. I lived with her and four other ballerinas. When I could support myself financially, I moved into a small apartment and lived there alone until I married Albert."

Shane looked from Annie's face to the shelved books and then to the albums on the trunk. He sat forward and reached for one. "May I?"

Shane could envision Annie, a beautiful young girl in a lonely life, her objective to dance, to please an audience, and her husband. When had she enjoyed a life of her own, until now, collecting her shells and stones for her garden?

"Of course," she said. "They're just old albums from my dancing life."

Shane opened the thick volume and found himself looking at a silhouette of a beautiful ballerina and, across from that photograph, a poster with ornate letters spelling out Annasheeva in brilliant red. "You?" he asked, holding the album so that she could see.

"Yes."

"Annasheeva?"

"Yes."

Shane smiled at Annie. "You're name is Annasheeva?"

Annie squirmed just a bit and placed her coffee cup down on the table next to her. "It was my stage name. The director I lived with thought that Anne Snow was not dramatic enough for an up and coming dancer – we melded together my mother's name, Eva, my grandmother's name, Sheila, and my own name. I became Annasheeva."

Shane stared at her. She was Annie.

He looked through the album laden with old tickets, small flyers announcing her performances, and an abundance of photos taken at every angle. She was amazing in her agility and grace, a magical figure in one impossible pose after another, spotlights causing part of her body to be illuminated and part of it to remain in shadow. Who was this before him?

When he closed the album, he looked at her for several moments without a word between them.

"Would you like another coffee?" she asked.

Shane didn't reply; he had no immediate words.

"I have cold drinks," she offered. "Lemonade, and there's wine in one of the cupboards."

"No, I'm fine. Thank you." He continued to survey her face, her slim body and bare feet. "Am I staying too long? What time do you go to bed?"

Annie laughed. "No, you're not staying too long at all. I'm enjoying having someone other than Daisy to talk to. I'm up most nights until midnight. I watch the news. If I can't alter the world issues, I go to bed."

Shane smiled as he placed the album back on the trunk. This woman was filled with charm from her lips as well as her gentle demeanor.

"Were you a demanding diva?" he teased.

Annie laughed. "Hardly."

Shane watched her, the way her eyes closed for a moment then opened to be focused on him.

"Did you love it?"

Annie's face reflected a slightly sad smile. "I didn't hate it. I suppose I liked the classes when I was small, but then I was left with the director to live in the big city, New York, and even though the house was home to four other dancers, and the director was kind, I was lonely for my real home in the Connecticut hills, my cats and chickens." Annie looked away and then back at Shane. "It was okay. I had a good life."

Shane's eyes went from Annie to the album then back to Annie. So much of her was in that collective keepsake, and most likely in the other beneath it. And yet he felt that there was more of Annie sitting before him on a simple sofa in a small cottage than there had ever been on a prominent New York stage or in a large house with servants.

"Do you still dance?" he asked. "I mean just to please yourself here in your home?"

Annie shook her head. "No, I'm not in the proper condition these days. I walk the beach to sooth my aching feet and ankles."

He nodded. "I can't imagine having to bend my feet so that I'm standing on my toes. It must hurt."

"It's certainly difficult to do at first, but it's gradual. Your feet and legs comply. Now that my dancing days are over, my body is learning to adjust – it's all a compromise."

"When did you stop dancing?"

"I danced until I was near forty. When parts became scarce for older dancers, I thought I'd retire and go back to school. Albert talked me into teaching ballet at a prestigious academy. I did that until I lost him a few years ago."

"And then you came here."

Annie nodded. "I sold the house in New York and cut ties, yes, and I came here. This," she said as she looked around the room, "suits me."

He understood; Annie had found a shelter. For the first time in her life, she had control over what time she went to sleep and what she did with her day. Her tastes for life were humble, satisfied with simple treasures from the sea and quiet hours with Daisy, who was now curled up next to her on the sofa.

Shane stood with obvious stiffness in his legs. "I should go," he said. "I want to be invited back."

Annie stood with her usual grace and perfect balance. She wanted to tell him that he could come back anytime, but she said nothing as they walked toward the door of the front porch. Shane reached for the door's handle as he thanked her again for supper, then he stumbled and she caught his arm to keep him from falling against the door jam.

Her hands on his left arm felt muscles. He was not a weak man, but injuries from Afghanistan had taken their toll. "Are you okay?" she asked, looking at his handsome face.

Shane smiled. "Yeah, except for my pride. Sorry about that. Every once-in-a-while I take a step and the hip and knee conspire to take me down."

Annie let go of his arm and stood back. "Are you going to be able to walk to the hotel?"

He assured her he'd be fine. "I'll bring my car next time, and I'll be moving into my apartment in a few days. Can't wait to have my own place now that the tourists have gone. So, tomorrow on the beach, around seven?"

Annie agreed to seven, but she worried as she watched him go. He had a quarter of a mile to walk.

She stood on the porch and watched him move, his figure fading away in the darkness, and only when she could not see him at all did she return to her living room. Her eyes caught sight of his jacket left across a chair. She touched it, picked it up, and held it close, then touched each metal snap as he had. Annie looked at the jacket as if it might speak to her, then she placed it back where he had left it. She would return it to him in the morning.

In the kitchen, she washed his bowl and coffee cup. She held his spoon a moment longer than she needed to as she washed it and left it to dry in the drainer. The little house felt very empty. Strange, she thought, how a person's spirit can penetrate a space and linger after they have gone.

Annie walked back into the living room and sat down, using the remote to turn on the eleven o'clock news. She watched and listened with half of her senses – the other half recalling the moments with Shane. She was anchored to him in a way in which she did not understand. *Was this unconditional love?* She wasn't sure in what capacity she cared for him. This was new.

When the news was over and the late night shows were on, Annie switched the TV and lights off. She gave Daisy a fresh bowl of water and went to her bedroom. With only the moonlight and a dim street light's glow, Annie slipped out of her clothing and into a knee-length nightgown. She slid beneath the sheets and stared at the ceiling. She'd enjoyed the evening, but why then did she feel isolated? Before Shane, she had moved about the town of Salt Hill Bay without thinking about who she would see. It never occurred to Annie who might see *her.* Fame meant nothing; it never had.

Chapter Five

While Annie's life had its routines, she diverted her daily tasks by treating herself to plucking flowers from her garden, bringing them inside to further enjoy. She watched for particular birds: Orioles and Scarlet Tanagers, Hummingbirds and Wrens. She planted what they would enjoy and bought birdseed with fruit in rich, red hues. She played soft classical music by Ravel and then changed to contemporary guitar pieces.

Shane's work allowed him hours at home on the computer, freedom to take a break when in pain and to take walks on the beach with Annie. His apartment was a vast improvement over the hotel room he had occupied for three months, but it was nothing anyone would call exquisite or even inviting. His kitchen was galley-style with barely enough room for a small refrigerator, electric stove, and sink. His living room became his office, and his bedroom was small and plain.

He thought about Annie often. Not certain what it was about her, other than her natural beauty. He could not escape; he envisioned her dancing. That she kept him at arm's length, he understood. It would be easy to fall in love with someone like her only to be rejected because of the difference in age. To him, Annie was ageless, but he thought to her he must seem unsophisticated.

On a Friday evening in mid-October they met at the

shore. It was just five-thirty and getting dark.

Annie kept her shoes on. The sand had a different coolness to it now, not soothing to her feet as it had been in the summer months. It began to feel penetratingly cold, yet yielding enough to provide a measure of comfort in walking. She wondered if it affected Shane in the same way.

"Getting dark earlier," he commented as they met at the rocks and stepped onto the sand.

"Yes. I don't like to see the sun go down so early, but this is New England and that's the deal."

"Ever think of moving, like to California, someplace always bright and warm?"

Annie shook her head. "No, I get used to each season; this is home."

Shane walked next to her, his eyes on the sea.

Before they reached their rock to sit, Shane stopped and Annie turned to look at him. She hesitated and then retraced her steps to stand closer. "Are you all right?"

Shane closed his eyes for a moment then opened them and took a deep breath.

"What's wrong, Shane? How can I help?"

He started to walk again but slowly. They reached the rock and sat down, the light growing dimmer, the tide coming in. Annie sat on the rock and took note of his profile. Shane was a handsome man.

"Sorry about that," he said.

"Don't apologize," she was quick to respond, "but I'm concerned about your pain. Have you seen a doctor recently?"

"Not for a while."

"Shouldn't you? I'm afraid you could be doing more damage to your injuries."

Shane brushed sand from his dark jeans. "They want

me to have a steel rod put in my leg and possibly go through surgery on my hip. I'm not ready for that."

Annie hesitated, not wanting to be too assertive. "Is this the VA? Are they the ones who want you to have this surgery?"

Shane squinted against the salt air and dimming light. "Yes. I had a lot of patching up done on my body. By the time I'd had three operations, I was ready to get out of there and home."

Annie was quiet. She understood. It was the same relief she'd felt in leaving New York and all the years of formal, step-by-step performing behind. She and Shane had found Salt Hill Bay and the undemanding style of life it offered.

"What happens to our walks once winter comes?" he asked.

"I walk around town," she said. "I need to keep these legs and feet nimble, and I like seeing life beyond my cottage. You get to know shop owners. They see you coming into the coffee shop for a muffin and they often have it bagged before you ever reach the counter to order."

Shane smiled. "That sounds pretty nice. Do they do that with you?"

"Sometimes. Ray at the bakery café is always ready with my hot tea, but he knows I alternate between a scone and a muffin. He waits for me to decide on that. And at the little grocery store, they know I'll be buying fruit – they get a double bag ready for me so that I won't lose those heavy items on my walk home."

"You don't have a car. Don't you miss that?"

Annie slid off the rock and Shane followed. "No. I learned to drive when I was twenty, but I never had a car. Living in New York, you really don't need one. Salt Hill

Bay has everything right here, and if I wanted to go a distance, I could rent a car."

Shane said nothing; he knew she had a point. "Well, if you ever want to borrow mine, you're welcome to it. And if you'd like to go someplace for a little get-a-way, I'd be happy to drive. We could head north to New Hampshire, or south to the Cape. It might be fun to have a day away."

Annie nodded. "That sounds nice. I'd like that."

Their steps back into town were made in silence except for the soft sounds of their feet against the sidewalk. At the corner where they usually parted, Shane looked at Annie, her blonde hair brushing softly against the red sweater buttoned up to her chin.

"Any chance we could do something this weekend? I feel like I'm shackled to my computer except for our walks on the beach. Let's go someplace for the day. Do you like antiques?"

"I love them," she was quick to reply.

"Great. Let's take a drive toward the Cape and check out some antique shops. We can have lunch along the way. I need some warmth in my apartment. I like copper, maybe a nice lantern would work, and some more comfortable chairs. I could use your help in selecting a few things. You need to see my place. It isn't much, but I think with a little dressing-up I can make it work."

"Tomorrow?" she asked.

"Sure, let's go tomorrow. What about our walk in the morning?"

Annie thought for a moment. "Let's skip it. If we head out early, around eight or nine, we could stop someplace for a little breakfast, my treat. And we'll do our walking in the antique shops."

Shane laughed. "Sounds good to me; I'll see you at

eight."

Annie walked toward home with that familiar fluttering feeling in her chest and abdomen. Spending time with Shane she would keep conversation simple, she would stay in the friend mode. She looked forward to the day with him, hunting for treasures.

Sorting through clothing she once wore in New York, she pulled a pair of slim-fitting black slacks and a shirt of pale gray silk from her closet. This would be comfortable for their excursion to the Cape.

With a glass of water in her hands, Annie walked into her living room and sat down. It had been a long time since she'd gone away for the day. Spending more than a couple of hours with Shane would be new, enjoyable, as well as tense. Annie rested her head back on the sofa and stared at the ceiling. What is it, she questioned herself, that I feel for him? *If we were the same age, yes, I could see myself with him. The bond is strong and sincere, but I don't know what it is.* And then she realized that the romantic spark wasn't there simply because she wouldn't allow it.

Annie took a few sips of her water then stood, turned out the lights, and went to the kitchen. She filled Daisy's water bowl and gave the cat a small amount of kibble until breakfast. Taking a deep breath, she left her glass in the sink, a nightlight on, and went to bed.

Morning brought an overcast sky. Still in her robe and slippers, Annie made coffee in her French press and noted that it was after seven. She quickly fed Daisy and dressed for her adventure with Shane. She felt excited about shopping. A minimalist in possessions, Annie decided that something new for the house, and maybe for her, would be invigorating. In New York, Albert had commissioned designers to visit their home where Annie would be invited to select style and fabric for coats, dresses, and even nightwear. The house had been tastefully furnished before she had married; there was nothing left to do, no sign of Annie in that space.

Dressed and her hair brushed, Annie sipped a cup of steaming coffee on her front porch. Moments after sitting down, Shane's car stopped right before her path to the front door.

"I can smell that coffee all the way out here," he said as he walked toward her porch.

Annie stood and opened the door for him. "Would you like some?"

"I would," he said as he walked up the two granite steps and into her home.

Annie turned to walk toward the kitchen. Shane followed her and she turned to see if he was okay; the steps seemed awkward for his leg and hip to navigate. She poured him a cup and handed it to him.

"Just what I needed," he said after a few swallows.

"Sit down," Annie invited.

She sat across from him and they were quiet as they both enjoyed the fresh brew.

He looked at her, the pale gold of her hair against the light gray of her shirt. She looked like a pastel painting from one of the old masters.

"You might bring a jacket. There's a chill in the air this morning."

"I noticed," she said. "I can't believe summer has gone past so quickly. I love all the seasons, but this summer seems to have flown. I'll get something to bring along." She stood and moved to her bedroom, returning wearing a russet colored sweater and carrying a small black purse over one shoulder.

Shane looked at her and wondered what he had here.

This woman was consistently beautiful, graceful, and composed. He wanted her in his life and wondered who wouldn't.

"Ready to go?" he asked, placing his cup in the sink.

"I am," she answered with an air of girlish enthusiasm in her voice.

As they made their way through the house to the front door, Shane leaned against the living room sofa.

"Are you all right?" Annie asked.

Shane stood as he took his hand from the sofa's arm. "I'm okay. This darn leg and hip are taking turns giving me a hard time."

"This is what you didn't get taken care of with your other injuries?"

"Right. By the time they'd patched up the ribs and collapsed lung, and a few other things, I didn't want the advised surgery on my knee and hip; might need to reconsider that at some point."

Annie stood motionless as he moved toward the door.

He turned around and looked at her solemn face. "All set to go?" he asked.

Annie felt tears form in her eyes and they did not go unnoticed.

"Annie, I'm okay. I've been hobbling around with this for a while now. Sometimes it wins for a minute or two. Come on; let's go find some neat stuff."

She moved toward him and while he stepped outside, she closed the porch door and locked it as she said goodbye to Daisy.

"So, off to the Cape with us," he said as he opened the car door for Annie. She slipped into the seat and strapped herself in, then watched as he did the same. Just moments on the road he looked at his passenger; she was taking in every detail of their journey.

"Do you have anything in mind you'd like to hunt for?" he asked.

"Not really. I'm looking forward to this though; maybe I'll find something I can't live without."

Shane smiled. "Are you still interested in stopping for breakfast at some point?"

"Yes, I'm starved," she said, wanting him to eat more than she felt the need for food herself.

With a hearty meal placed before them, they ate, drank more coffee, then eagerly made their way to the car and the open road.

Once over the bridge and the scenic blue canal below, the Cape loomed before them. They chose a back route winding through quaint towns and tree-studded streets. The first shop they came to was attached to a Cape Cod style home, its owner a woman certain to be in her late eighties or early nineties. She invited them to look around in the shop and to bring anything they were interested in to her door. They could bicker there, she told them, over a better price.

"Look at this," Shane said to Annie as he held a large copper lantern up for her to see. "I love copper; I can electrify this and make a neat lamp for my place."

Annie walked closer to him and touched the clasp on the lantern door. "This is in great condition," she said. "I like it."

"What's that in your hand?" he asked.

Annie moved her fingers and exposed a pair of earrings in her palm.

Shane looked at them and then took one from her, holding it up to the light. "Wow, that's a nice color. Magenta?"

"I'd say so. I love the way the glass, whatever it is, reflects the light."

Shane moved the hair covering her left ear and in doing so barely touched her skin with his fingertips. Annie shivered and hoped he hadn't noticed.

"I never observed you wearing earrings before. The ones you have on are beautiful; they look like diamonds."

Annie was quiet as she studied the brilliant earring he placed back in her hand.

"What other kinds of earrings do you like?" he asked.

Annie touched the diamond on her left side. "These are all I have. Albert gave them to me and said nothing else could ever compare."

Shane wasn't sure what to say to that remark. It felt to him that Albert, even with his obvious adoration for Annie, could be controlling.

"So, are you thinking of getting these?" He looked at the contents of her dainty hand.

"Yes, I think I will."

Before they left the shop, Shane found a hammer he liked, the wooden handle a rich patina; Annie found a large basket and an additional pair of lapis blue earrings.

They laughed as they packed their new found belongings in the trunk of Shane's car, each of them delighted with having found treasures to take home. Their next stop was just a few miles further down the Cape road at a small shop featuring used books. They spent an hour looking through old pages and admiring the bindings and covers. Shane ended up purchasing a huge, beautifully bound book containing old front pages of London newspapers. Annie found a small volume of poetry by John Greenleaf Whittier, its cover depicting a young girl in a flowing pink dress.

"Lunch?" Shane asked as they slid into the seats of his car.

"Oh," Annie said, "are we through with our shopping?"

Shane laughed. "You should see the look on your face. That was a pout if I ever saw one. No, I thought we'd have a little something to eat and then we can shop some more."

Annie fastened her seat belt as they pulled back onto the road taking them further south. She glanced at his profile. His eyes were beautiful but there was a sadness in the way he half shielded them with lids laden with generous lashes. He was an outstanding young man; Annie thought he should be out with a young woman he cared for. She thought about her feelings for him; they were growing deeper, and yet she wanted more for him than a woman old enough to be his mother. She wanted him to find a great love and to have a full life, perhaps with children. She would be genuinely happy for him while understanding that she would mourn the loss of their closeness.

The scenery before them was of old roads, old trees, and at several points along the winding route, glimpses of the sea. Annie couldn't remember a time in her life when so much colorful beauty presented itself to her; and neither could she recall a deeper feeling of contentment. There was a comfort in being with Shane.

He stole glances at her when his eyes caught the movement of her head turning to the window on her right. She was beautiful, physically and in her tranquility. No one had ever affected him in this way. He thought about her dancing, the spotlight on her body, every move needing to be exact. An audience darkened so that to Annie, it must have felt as if she was alone. Her life had its share of being unique with fame and certainly ample funds, but he wondered how happy she had been.

The woman beside him seemed more a girl than his own younger sister.

After a brief stop for lunch in a small roadside café, they traveled further south until they came to another charming antique shop. They started out looking at objects together, then Annie went to a display of jewelry clumped together in a large tray while Shane searched through a collection of old tools. After twenty minutes, he returned to her side and watched as she scrutinized the earrings amidst the jewelry. In her hand she held two pair: one of topaz set in gold and another pair in silver leaves.

"What do you have there?" he asked, knowing already that she held earrings.

"I like these," she said, holding them closer for him to see. "And what did you find?"

Shane showed her an old wrench, a pair of pliers, and a copper kettle. "Aren't these great?"

With their treasures in hand, they made their way from the shop to the car then headed northward to Salt Hill Bay. It was almost four in the afternoon when they arrived back at Annie's house. Shane parked the car but did not shut off the engine. They looked at one another and then they laughed.

"I had a wonderful time today," she said. "Thank you so much, Shane."

"I thank you," he said. "I'd never have done this on my own; it wouldn't have been the same. Are we walking tonight?"

Annie put her head back on the car's seat and smiled. "I think I feel lazy. I may wait and walk in the morning."

"Sounds good to me," he said as he started to get out of the car.

"No, stay," she said. "You must be tired, too. See you

in the morning; maybe at seven-thirty?"

"You've got it," he said, "but I need to retrieve your purchases."

Annie smiled and waited as he opened the car's trunk. When Annie heard his car pull away, she didn't turn to watch. Inside the house she greeted Daisy then left her small packages in a chair. She went to the kitchen to feed the cat and heat some coffee, slipped out of her shoes, and walked into her bedroom where she hesitated before changing clothes. The day had been like no other, filled with fun. I want more of feeling this way, she thought. Even though she knew in her heart that this was an impossible and improbable relationship, unreasonable in many ways, Annie loved possessing Shane in the moment.

Chapter Six

The chill of the coming season, darker mornings and evenings, changed the timing for Annie's and Shane's walks. One morning in late October, as they concluded their beachside stroll, shoes on, walking in barely damp sand, Shane reached out for Annie's hand and clasped it firmly as they made their way over rocks to the town's sidewalk.

"Tonight," he said, "after our walk, I'd like you to come to dinner. I'll pick you up."

Annie swallowed hard. "Why tonight?"

Shane kept his eyes on hers. "No being reluctant," he said. "Tonight you will dine on my famous lasagna. It's good, I promise. I'll zip home after we walk, turn the oven on, and then I'll be back to drive you to my place. I've been wanting you to see it. I have the copper lantern all wired; it has a nice glow. The copper kettle sits on my stove, very appropriate. You can't say no."

Annie slipped her hand from his and buttoned her light jacket against the morning breeze.

"So," he continued, "would our walk be okay for around four? That would give us daylight and then I could be back to collect you around six-thirty."

Annie looked to the sea and then at Shane. His handsome face expressed enthusiasm she found difficult to resist. "Okay. I'll see you at the rocks."

Shane nodded as he tucked his hands into his jean pockets.

She took a few steps backward then turned toward her house.

Shane watched her go, a sense of resignation in her stride. He squinted against the sun; even from the back, she was breathtakingly graceful to watch.

Annie entered her home and greeted Daisy with a deep sigh. "How did I get cornered into this?" At that point, she sat down on her sofa, jacket still on buttoned to her throat. She thought about the men in her life. Her father had been kind, but firm and distant. Her first boyfriend when she was thirteen was a Russian dancer she worked with. He was fourteen and had declared his love for Annie. For three years she thought about him kissing her and he never had. When he was seventeen, for reasons she did not know, he returned to Russia. Annie felt lost and her interest in boys waned with his leaving. There were few opportunities for romance when practice and performing took much of her life, then Albert invited her to dinner. As the maestro she thought he wanted to speak with her about the music for a coming production. She was surprised and flattered when he made it clear that he was interested in her as a woman – she was barely twenty-one, he was thirty-six. It would be two years of courtship, formal and proper, before they were married in New York.

On a brief trip home to see her family before the small, elegant wedding, it was Annie's mother who questioned the age difference between her daughter and intended husband. She suggested that Albert seemed a bit controlling, insisting that the marriage take place in the city rather than in Annie's Connecticut home town. Annie had defended his choice. In order to have the majority of the dance company's members attend, they would need to make the ceremony convenient.

Two years before Albert passed away, Annie's mother died in her sleep. She had been hiding an illness for years and succumbed to it quietly, as she had lived. Now Annie thought about the fact that Albert, kind as he was, did make most of the decisions for both of them, even to not having a child. Was she falling into this arrangement again with Shane? Was he making decisions for both of them, as in the unexpected dinner invitation?

Annie stood and unbuttoned her jacket, shaking it off and hanging it in her front closet. She walked into her bedroom and looked at her wardrobe, wondering what she would wear to dine with Shane. She selected a simple ankle length dress in deep blue and an ecru sweater to wear over it.

After their late afternoon walk, Annie changed into her dress and brushed her hair. For the first time in years, she took the diamond earrings from her ears and placed them carefully in the small box in which they had arrived. She inserted the blue lapis earrings in place, liking the way they complimented the blue of her dress. *Am I letting go of Albert?* The thought made her wonder. He had been kind and generous – she understood that his seemingly controlling manner was his way of showing compassion. He had done everything possible to provide his wife with a charmed, calm existence. Although some it must have seemed he managed her life, he had contrived to take care of her. His "little bird," he sometimes teasingly referred to her, must surely require guardianship in a safe nest.

Shane arrived promptly at six-thirty and met Annie as she was halfway down her front path. A bottle of wine in her hand, she slipped into his car. At his apartment in an old wood structure at the northern part of town, Annie found the place appealing, so much like buildings in her home town. Shane's apartment was on the second of three floors, and while it was old and the wide pine floors were slightly warped, the place was spacious, adorned with crown moldings and chair rails around the rooms.

"Home sweet home," he said as he took her sweater and hung it carefully in a closet. He invited her to sit or browse the area while he fetched two glasses and chilled wine.

Annie walked around a sparsely furnished living room which had a non-working fireplace at one wall. Shane's lit copper lantern sat perched on the mantle near a comfortable looking old chair. Opposite the hearth, a sofa was positioned. She walked to the door of his bedroom. The wallpaper was a pale blue background with pink flowers. She smiled, certain that this was not Shane's choice. When she turned from that room, she walked toward the kitchen where Shane pulled the pan of lasagna from the oven to set while they had wine.

"It smells very good," she said.

"I'm not a bad cook," he replied as he placed the filled wine glass in her hands. "And I have a nice salad and Italian bread to go with it. Would you like to sit for a bit? The lasagna needs a few minutes to cool down."

Annie moved to a single chair as Shane sat down on the sofa's center cushion.

"Your apartment is very nice, Shane. The rooms are larger than those in my cottage."

Shane looked around. "It's not nearly as nice as your place, but it's comfortable. A few more trips to antique shops should bring in some coziness. I'd like a few more pieces of copper."

Their conversation was light and dinner was, as promised, delicious.

Annie's fears for a date-like evening were unfounded. Shane was a relaxed host and seemed proud to have his friend in his home. He pointed out the architectural benefits of living in an older building. There was never a moment of awkward silence or physical closeness. He sensed her apprehension and was determined to make this evening the first and not the last.

When a clock in the living room struck eleven, Annie was amazed that the time had passed so quickly. "I should go," she said as she stood. "I can walk from here, Shane; it's not that far."

"No way," he said. "I would never have you walking at night by yourself. I'll get your sweater and I'll drive you back to Daisy."

Annie followed him toward the closet. "She has this penetrating way of looking at me when I've been out, even for my daily walks."

Shane draped the sweater carefully over Annie's shoulders as she slipped her arms into the sleeves. Again his fingers brushed the skin at her neck and he quickly moved his hands away.

The drive to her cottage was uneventful, filled with her thanks to him for a wonderful meal and good company. At her door, they didn't touch. They said goodnight and agreed to meet at seven in the morning for their walk on the shore.

Inside, Annie took a few deep breaths and walked to her bedroom. There, everything she had on her body came off and was replaced with a light jersey nightgown down to her knees. She sat on the side of her bed, Daisy joining her. She leaned forward, her hands against her knees, and wondered how she'd been able to get through this night. She restrained herself from simply reaching out to touch Shane's sweet face or taking his hand in hers. Something inside of her wanted to assure him that he would be okay. He needed to finish whatever treatment was needed - she would help him. It pained her to know that he was in discomfort from his injuries, and she knew from her dancer's body, as age progressed, so would the agony.

She stood and walked to the kitchen for a glass of water, turned off lights, and sat down in the darkened living room. Where was she going with this relationship? It was with fear that she asked herself this question time after time. Shane Bellows was important to her, but he wasn't hers. At some point she would need to let go and the fright came from not understanding how she would accomplish that brutal task.

Annie had mirrors. She knew that her looks had been a lifelong asset as a performer, and that Albert had found her irresistible – it had been nothing she instigated or protected, it was who she was and how she'd been born, fortunate to be attractive. No woman Shane became involved with would tolerate Annie in his life, even with the difference in age.

Feeling a chill, she moved from the sofa to her bed. Daisy gave her a scrutinizing look, as if accusing Annie of disturbing her sleep. Annie reached out to pat the cat gently then she slipped her feet beneath the covers. She pulled the sheet, blanket, and coverlet up to her chin, glad to be where the warmth was already enveloping her body.

Chapter Seven

Each day came with expectations. They would meet and walk the shoreline or in town. Each evening would bring the same, and then one evening, it did not. Annie waited at the rocks for Shane until it grew dark. She glanced toward the sea, its surface blackened with autumn sunset, and then she turned toward town. Lights were flowing through the main street and she started to walk. After no more than a few hundred yards, Annie stopped, turned around, and headed home. Something was wrong; she would call Shane to see why he wasn't there.

By the time she arrived back home and had left her jacket over a chair, Annie felt almost frantic about Shane's whereabouts and condition. Often she'd noted that his walking was slower, his gait less steady.

"Shane," she said into the phone as he answered, "are you okay?"

There was a distinct hesitation from him and then his weakened voice. "Sorry, Annie; I called your house but you must have left. I'm okay."

Annie took a deep breath. "You don't sound okay."

Again a brief hesitation before he replied. "The old knee and hip are giving me a little grief," he said. "I'm hanging out on the sofa for a while."

Annie sat in a chair and closed her eyes for a moment. "Have you had dinner?"

"No, but I'm not all that hungry. I'll get something later."

Annie stood and walked with the phone in her hand to the kitchen. She had tomato bisque soup and a hearty bread. "I'm walking over there," she said. "I have some nice soup I made earlier today."

"Annie, don't. It's cold and dark."

"I'm fine; I go out walking in this sort of weather and dark all the time. I'll be there in about twenty minutes."

Shane held the phone to his lips and closed his eyes as he heard Annie's phone click away.

This wasn't how he wanted her to visualize him. She had this enduring beauty, and with his physical issues, what did he have to give in return?

Annie shed a steady stream of tears as she gathered what she needed to take to Shane. This was unlike him; she feared for his physical and mental well-being. With the soup, bread, and three Macintosh apples in a bag, she dressed warmly and began her walk. Every step she took was with thoughts of Shane and how she would find him. Not even Albert's slow illness and eventual death had shattered her to this extent. Shane was young – he should have his whole life ahead of him. As she walked, she prayed softly, "Let him mend. Please, let him mend."

True to her word, Annie arrived at Shane's to find his door unlocked. He was stretched out on the sofa, struggling to sit up as she entered. He seemed, she thought, flustered with her arrival, apologetic for his troubles. Without a word, she walked to him and set her bag on his coffee table as she slipped out of her jacket.

His face was pale.

She tried to say his name but swallowed back tears and anxiety instead. There was no doubt, he was in pain.

"Annie," he said, "don't look so concerned. This isn't

the first time I've felt beaten down. It's been a while, but I've been here once or twice."

"You're in pain," she said.

"Yeah, I am."

"What do you have?"

"Aspirin. I've used up the other stuff."

Annie took a deep breath. "Will you eat a little soup before I take you to the hospital?"

Shane sat up straighter. "What hospital?"

"I'll drive you to the local one; it's just a few miles from here. Can you eat just a little soup before we go?"

"Annie, I don't want to go. I'll be okay."

She stood straight and then took the bag to the kitchen. In his microwave, she heated a small portion of the soup and brought it to him, sitting next to him on the sofa. "You need this," she said. "The emergency room will be busy – we'll have a wait, but you need something, Shane. Your face is white with agony."

With just a few sips of hot soup and another few sips of water, Annie helped him into a jacket. She slipped her own back on and asked for his car keys.

"You sure you can drive?" he asked.

"I'm sure. Come on, Shane. You need some help."

They made their way out of his apartment, down to his car, then to the hospital's emergency room. Seeing how pale and weak he was, a nurse took him inside immediately for treatment.

Annie sat anxiously in the waiting room, convinced that Shane might be staying the night.

When the nurse brought him back in a wheel chair an hour later, she spoke to Annie as if she was Shane's wife.

"He's been given a shot to make him more comfortable and tomorrow you'll need to get this prescription filled. It's for pain. There's only enough for three days. He needs to see his doctors at the Veteran's Hospital for further treatment. We've explained all of this to Mr. Bellows."

Annie looked at his face as she accepted the written prescription. Shane looked down toward his feet and then up to her with a smile. "Got yourself a winner, didn't you?"

Annie could feel the traitorous tears forming and she looked away. "You're going to see the doctors at the VA this time, Shane. For now, I'll take you home."

She thanked the nurse as he was wheeled to the car. There, Annie helped him into the passenger seat where he was looking more comfortable than he had en-route to the hospital.

"Thank you," he said as Annie steered the car out of the parking lot and back toward the town's center.

"I'm stopping at your apartment, Shane, to collect some clothes. Can you tell me what you'd like to have with you?"

"You're taking me to the VA tonight?"

"No. I'm taking you to my place tonight and to the VA tomorrow. Where will I find your pajamas and anything else you'll need?"

Shane slid further down into the passenger seat as would a child when told he was going to the doctor. Annie looked at him and asked again where she could find his basic needs. Shane sat up straight and told her which bureau drawers held clothes he'd require and what in the bathroom he would need.

"Annie," he said as they pulled into his apartment's parking lot, "I'll be fine here tonight."

Annie ignored his statement. She was quiet as she parked the car, left the engine on, and went quickly to his apartment. She returned with an overnight bag and tossed it into the back seat without a word.

At her house, Annie held Shane's arm as she carried the overnight bag into her living room. She set it down and helped him out of his jacket. He started to sit down on the sofa when she stopped him. "No," she said, "you're better off in my guest room. It's all made up; you'll be comfortable there. That shot they gave you could make you drowsy – the bathroom is between your room and mine. Would you like anything? Tea, water, juice - something to eat?"

Shane laughed. "You're quite the little drill sergeant."

Annie knew her strengths – when there was an emergency, she didn't shy away from it. This was an emergency in her mind, getting Shane back into the shape a man of his age should be.

With her guest settled into bed, Annie again asked if there was anything he needed. Shane gave her a half smile and said that he was all set. Annie shut his bedroom door then leaned against it in the hallway; her eyes closed, she took a deep breath. Never had any man spent the night with her, not since Albert.

After a few moments, Daisy came along and Annie was fearful that the cat would start meowing, questioning the guest room door being closed. Annie moved down the hall toward the kitchen, softly calling Daisy who turned and followed.

When morning came Annie realized that after several hours awake, she had slept. She reached for her wristwatch and saw that it was near seven. Pushing the covers aside, she swung her legs out of bed and sat there thinking about what to do first. She slipped into jeans and a loose shirt then made her way to Shane's room. She listened at the door and heard nothing.

"Shane?" she said softly.

"Come on in, Annie."

Annie hesitated then turned the doorknob and walked into his room. He was in bed, the sheet and one blanket pulled up to his chest.

"How are you this morning?" she asked, moving closer to him.

"Not too bad," he said. "Thanks to you."

"I'm going to fix some eggs. Do you need help getting dressed?"

Shane gave her a smile. "Yes to eggs, no to getting dressed, thank you. I'll be out in a few minutes."

Annie moved, taking a few steps backward, then turned and left his room. In the kitchen she started scrambled eggs then fed Daisy. Coffee and toast were ready at just about the time Shane entered the room and said that everything smelled great.

Their conversation was sparse, but Annie was firm when she asked, "Ready to go?"

Shane looked at her as he brushed a napkin across his lips.

"Where are we going?"

"I looked up the number for the nearest VA Hospital. We need to go into Boston. They have access to your records; they'll see you today before noon."

Shane squinted against the idea of going but knew he had come to the point where he could no longer deny the pain.

"Wouldn't it be easier if I took a cab? I'm sure you have more to do than drive in and out of Boston."

Annie shook her head. "No. I'd like to drive you if you'll allow me the use of your car. The front desk gave me directions; it's right off the highway, so it won't be a problem."

Within an hour, overnight bag in tow, Shane slipped

into the passenger seat as Annie made herself comfortable behind the wheel. Morning traffic was aggravatingly slow, but by ten o'clock they were walking into the lobby of the gigantic hospital. This was the part that brought the reality of Shane's injuries front and center. Annie swallowed hard as they walked into the building where she knew things were about to change. There would be no morning and evening walks at the shore or through town. There would be no pleasant dinners together and shopping for antiques for quite a while. The future was unknown and to be feared. The most feared part was Shane's recovery – that he could be mended and whole again. Annie was frightened within, recalling those last weeks with Albert, watching a strong man become weak and pained. It was something she hoped never to see again.

Her feelings for Shane were intrinsically beyond anything she had ever known; uncertain where the compassion for him was rooted, she only understood that his body needed to heal, and she would accept her role in that healing.

Leaving him there after admittance was the hardest part. She stayed until they suggested she leave in order for them to perform their tests. She wanted to reach out to him, to hug him. She smiled at him and told him he'd be well soon and that she would be back to visit each day.

Fighting traffic and parking woes in the city, Annie never missed an opportunity to spend time at Shane's side. They operated on his leg, inserting a steel rod. They operated on his shattered hip, and they gave him injections to prompt his body to mend and feel stronger. It was a matter of three weeks before he was moved to a facility for therapy. After five weeks there, and just two weeks before Christmas, Annie drove Shane back to Salt Hill and tried not to cry by pointing out the decorations mounted to lanterns and trees.

At a stop light near his apartment she asked, "Should we pick up some more of your clothes and other belongings?"

Shane looked surprised. "I thought I'd be going back to *my* place."

"With the stairs to climb, I thought you might be better staying with me for a few days. I only have the two granite steps into the house. I'll do whatever you want, Shane. I won't be abandoning you – I expect to stay with you whether it's at your place or mine. They wouldn't have let you home unless I promised to watch after you closely."

Shane closed his eyes and then opened them again. He looked at Annie as she navigated the streets bustling with shoppers.

"Okay," he said, "I'll stay with you if you'll have me. I'm really sorry about this, Annie. I feel like a real pain in the …"

"You're not," she said. "I'm sure that if the tables were turned, you'd be doing this for me. Besides, Daisy is going to love an extra lap."

She glanced over at her passenger long enough to trade smiles with him.

They stopped briefly at Shane's apartment for a few extra items of clothing and his laptop so that he could continue his work then went on to Annie's house. Getting him comfortably out of the car was not an easy task, but slowly, carefully, they managed the move until Shane could maneuver his body to the sofa.

"I'm going to get you one of your pain meds," she said. "It's time, and then I'll heat you some coffee." She wanted to add that he would see improvement every day, but she decided to keep promises at a minimum.

With nutritious food and medicine delivered on schedule, Shane found part of each day was best spent stretched out in his bed. Therapy was provided at home three days each week. With trembling fingers, Annie needed to change the dressing on his hip daily. Embarrassed at first, Shane closed his eyes as Annie removed bandages, used a cleansing solution, and applied the medication as she'd been directed by the hospital staff, and redressed the six-inch incision.

"I'm going out to get us a surprise," Annie announced one week before Christmas.

Shane smiled as he lowered his body carefully to the sofa where Annie had left coffee on the table next to him.

"What are you up to?" he teased.

"You'll see," she said, slipping her arms into a hip-length black coat. "I'll be right back, and I'm bringing us some food; any interest in Thai?"

"That sounds really good. My wallet is in my room. Please, at least let me contribute to the food budget."

"Not this time," she said. "When you're well, we'll go out for dinner and I'll order something extravagant to make you feel better."

Shane laughed. "Okay, you've got a deal."

Annie went out and returned with an assortment of Thai food and a three-foot high Christmas tree. Shane struggled to his feet, complimenting her on the shape of the beautiful little spruce. Annie placed the rooted tree in a silver pail she'd left by the door. She told him that she would add water once they'd had their meal.

"Do we have decorations?" Shane asked as Annie walked to the kitchen.

"Yes," she said, "we do." She thought about the huge

ten-foot tree Albert insisted on having each year in their New York home and the small portion of decorations she had brought with her to this tiny house.

Shane rested his head on the sofa's back and thought about Christmas. Two of them spent in Afghanistan, the one before Salt Hill Bay at his family's home in Pennsylvania. Injuries aside, he was looking forward to this Christmas with Annie, then he wondered how he was going to manage a gift for her. He went on line in search of jewelry, finding silver shell earrings.

Christmas morning was crisp and bright; snowflakes made a scattered appearance like glimmering diamonds in the sun. Before the decorated tree in the living room, Annie served breakfast with homemade muffins on the side. With a second cup of coffee, she placed a wrapped box on Shane's lap and said, "Merry Christmas, Shane."

His eyes clouded with her gentle and thoughtful behavior as he looked at the package. He stood just enough to take a tiny package from his jeans pocket, placing it in her hands.

His gift was a gray zipper-front sweater, a shade darker than the color of his eyes. He slipped his arms into it and told her how much he loved it. Annie opened her earrings and failed to stop the traitorous tears.

"They're perfect," she said as she fastened the shells in place.

Chapter Eight

Shane received therapy for eight weeks, with orders to walk. He was told to move slowly but to maintain the routine on a daily basis. Annie was more than willing to accompany him into the deep cold of early March. Shane was eager to move in spite of his discomfort; the promise of a warm drink at the end of each morning's session helped.

"What would I do without you?" he asked her one morning over coffee in their favorite café.

Annie smiled. "You'd have managed. I'm sure your family would have been eager to help you if you'd gone to them."

Shane had a wistful look. "Maybe."

Annie didn't ask what he implied. She had the feeling that while his family was important to him, there were unresolved differences.

Their walks through the streets of town were slow and time-planned so that Shane would not over-exert himself. He was gaining some needed weight and Annie was glad for that. He was definitely on the mend.

"I was thinking," he said as they finished a walk and were entering Annie's house, "that I might like to see how I do on the stairs at my place. I love living with you, but it's been a long time. I think I should get out of your hair and see about taking care of myself."

Annie hadn't expected the division to come so soon. She swallowed and forced a smile. "I've enjoyed having you, but if you'd like to try getting back on your own, I'd be glad to drive you to your apartment tomorrow. We'll need to get you a few grocery items too. Let's give it a try."

While her heart was breaking, she was thrilled with Shane feeling well enough to make it on his own. She would check on him. She would do what he needed, and she would stay out of his life unless he requested her presence.

"Don't think you're getting away from me. If the stairs are doable, I'll stay there and you'll come to visit, every day, right?"

Annie looked down at her feet and then up into his beautiful eyes. "Let's see how you're doing on your own. But yes, I'll visit and help in any way you need me."

"I'll always need you, Annie."

Those few words from Shane held great meaning. He wasn't teasing; he was serious and it felt a little awkward. She wanted to ask if they would continue their walks. She said nothing.

That evening Annie felt almost weak preparing their last evening meal at her cottage. She baked potatoes the way he liked them, adding in butter, sour cream, pepper, and salt. She would tell him how to make them, or maybe not. She would think more about that later. Right then all Annie wanted to do was cry. She hated the last of anything.

That evening there was a silence between them as they watched TV. Annie tried to read a book as she watched, but her mind was cemented in what the morning would bring. She would take Shane to his apartment, leaving her small abode feeling empty and sad. It was, she was certain, going to be terrible.

Shane was quiet, too. Where he normally inserted a comment about something he saw at a news break, he was still.

When the eleven o'clock news was over, Shane stood and said that he thought he'd go to bed. Annie nodded and said goodnight. She watched as Daisy hopped off the sofa and followed Shane to his room. With her head back against her chair, Annie could feel the tears warm against her skin. She wiped them away and started to get up when Shane walked back into the room.

He looked at her and then moved toward her. "Hey," he said softly, "what's going on here?"

Annie coughed and stood up straight. "Nothing, just swallowed the wrong way."

Shane looked at her, his hands on his hips. "You sure you're okay?"

Annie nodded. "Yes, I'm fine. Did you need something?"

Shane looked at her beautiful, tear-stained face. "I just wanted to say thank you, Annie, for everything. I'm going to miss this." And then, to add a touch of humor he said, "That cat is going to miss me. I'll have to stop by to see her every now and then."

Annie smiled. "You'll always be welcome."

"And we'll still go for our usual walks, right?"

Annie hesitated. "If you're up for the walks, yes, certainly."

"We can call each other to coordinate our time."

"Yes," she said. "We'll do that."

Shane looked at Annie for several silent seconds. His words weren't there, but the intensity in his eyes revealed his longing.

Annie caught the look and glanced away, embarrassed

to note his attraction and her own deep feelings.

"Have a good night's sleep," she said softly to dismiss him.

Without a word, Shane turned and walked slowly back to his room.

There was something Annie knew of herself, that it was both childish and selfish that she wanted two things at the same time: she wanted Shane to be well and independent, but she also wanted him to stay. She rubbed her eyes softly, stood, turned off the two lamps, and left the room in darkness. That's the way she felt: dark inside with sadness for what she had always known she could not keep.

After a simple breakfast, Annie drove him home. There was a light rain, but otherwise Shane's move back into his apartment occurred without incidence. Holding onto one bannister, he maneuvered the stairs slowly, each step secure. Annie watched him from behind, pleased that he had no sign of discomfort, no visual weakness. At the top of the stairs, he turned to her and smiled.

"I nailed it," he said.

Annie smiled and followed him into his apartment. He turned the heat up and left an overnight bag on a chair, shedding his jacket. Annie placed his laptop bag on the coffee table and the additional overnight bag in his room then looked at his barren kitchen. "We'll need to get you some groceries." Shane walked into the kitchen and opened the refrigerator. Bottled water, a few bottles of beer, relish, and mustard stared back at them. He then opened a cupboard. "Ah," he said, "I have plenty of coffee, and look at this, good old-fashioned spaghetti in a can." He smiled at her and said that he'd pick up some fresh food in the morning.

"You haven't driven in months. Would you like me to drive you to a store tomorrow?"

"Yes," he said, "I would, but only because I want you to take my car home now so you don't have to walk in this weather. Come back when you're ready tomorrow. We can shop and then maybe take a little walk. How would that work for you?"

Annie nodded. "That would be fine," she said softly.

Driving back to her cottage, Annie felt the deepest sense of loneliness that she had ever known. Losing Albert had been a process with his illness. It had been life-altering and yet a relief to set him free from suffering. Now she questioned herself in a thousand ways, wondering exactly what her life without Shane would entail. Life had become incredibly complicated with this uninvited emotion. Love; she knew it was love.

Here was the decision left in her way. From a child, she was firmly instructed for dance and life with a schedule. As an adult, Albert had taken over her life, seeing to her routine at ballet, her clothing, her comfort. Annie's first decision on her own was selling the New York house and moving to Salt Hill Bay and her little cottage near the sea. Now she was confronted once more with how to handle her own heart. Much would need to stay unspoken, a silent love.

She parked Shane's car in front of her home and walked into the small house to be greeted by Daisy. The cat looked at her and then beyond her as if to question the whereabouts of her friend.

Annie sank down onto the sofa, her jacket still on, and fell asleep. When she opened her eyes, she remembered. She was alone. Daisy walked to her side with questions in her eyes as Annie stood, removed her jacket, and walked to the kitchen. Daisy followed and sat by her bowl as dinner was served.

Annie went about robotically doing what needed to be done. She thought about changing the sheets in Shane's room but she chose to leave it as it was. She felt weak with the idea of entering the room where once he had been, recovering, sleeping. Her mind told her to function. She was directed by an inner force to do what needed to be done without hesitation for sorrow or self-pity.

The next morning, Annie showered, changed, and went to Shane's apartment. He needed groceries; that was first on her list.

He greeted her at the door with a vibrant smile. "Hey, I made it. Look at me, a whole person again, and I have you to thank."

Annie stepped inside his apartment. "You look strong."

"I feel strong, I really do, Annie. I was sinking when I met you and look what you've done. Come on; let's go for a walk, then breakfast and some shopping. Are you up for that?"

"Sure," she said, happy to witness his enthusiasm.

Their walk was fast-paced, filled with an energy Annie had never known in Shane. As they stepped over the incline of rocks at the shore, he reached out for her hand. She took it, glad not to worry negotiating the stones that were prone to moving beneath her feet.

When they reached the sand, she started to withdraw her hand as usual, but Shane's grasp tightened and he didn't let go until Annie moved enough to create a two-foot gap between them.

"So, did Daisy miss me last night?" he asked as he tucked his hands into his trouser pockets.

Annie smiled and looked to the sea. "I think she did, yes."

Shane looked at her and teased, "And what about you? Did you miss me last night?"

Annie looked as far down the beach as her eyes could see and withheld a comment.

Shane smiled; he hadn't won that game. They walked the damp sand in silence for several minutes before they reached their rock. They started to sit when Shane placed his hand on the boulder and decided it was too cold to perch on. He reached out for Annie's jacket, tugged on it gently, and suggested they go for a nice breakfast at their café.

After eggs, toast, and coffee together, talking comfortably about Shane's computer work, they walked to Shane's apartment parking lot, slipped into the car, and drove two miles for groceries. Shane filled his cart with easy to prepare meals. Annie added tangerines, apples, salad greens, and chunks of butternut squash.

"You like these things," she said when he gave her a questioning look, "and they're good for you."

Days went by with similar routines. They walked and talked of what each one was doing. Shane's work was becoming a challenge; there was much of it to keep him busy. There were days when he didn't join her for a walk either morning or evening – he was too involved in finishing a particular project.

One evening when Annie had just returned from her walk through town in semi-darkness, Shane knocked on her door. She was surprised to see him, half fearful that something was wrong.

"Come in," she beckoned. "It's cold out there for April, but by the sea, I suppose, we should expect that added chill."

Shane walked in, spotted Daisy at the same time that the cat noticed him, and reached down to pick her up.

79

The show of affection from Daisy made Annie smile.

Shane rubbed his chin against the cat's head then sat down with her on his lap.

"Would you like coffee or something else warm to drink?"

Shane looked up from his feline admirer and smiled at Annie's offer. "Coffee would be terrific."

When she went into the kitchen, he followed, carrying Daisy until she squirmed to get down.

"I was wondering," he said, "about going for dinner tomorrow evening. I've been working so much, I need a break. I'd like to get back out for another antique hunt too. Are you game?"

Annie's heart skipped a beat; she hoped she wouldn't spill his coffee as she poured and then handed it to him. She agreed that dinner and antiquing would be something she'd enjoy, but she wondered how awkward it might be this time around. There was so much about this arrangement that felt both right and wrong at the same time.

When Shane went to his apartment that night, he went back to work. He had messages that he'd been assigned new accounts, one of them a famed ballet company in New York. He immediately thought of Annie, hesitated, then punched in her name.

Annasheeva came up immediately with multiple photos of her in varying positions for stage. He was breathless looking from one to the other, reading about her career, the talent credited to her as a performer and introvert. He couldn't take his eyes from her beauty, from her face, from who he knew her to be. *Annie. Annasheeva. So beautiful.* He sat back in his chair and stared at the screen. She was everywhere in his life and yet he'd felt her resistance.

Chapter Nine

With their morning walk and coffee to follow at the café, Shane asked about timing for their dinner out. "Does six work for you? I have some added work, so I probably won't walk later, but I'm looking forward to dinner. I'll pick you up."

Annie brushed muffin crumbs from her jacket. "Six would work."

She walked home with spirit in her steps. As much as she felt apprehension in being with him, she felt the longing and pure joy of knowing that he sought her companionship. For whatever reason he had, as her nephew, her friend, she didn't care. He was in her life and that was all she required to completely fill her heart.

She thought back to the life she'd lived – it had all been filled with activity determined by others, and she had not experienced the time to develop her own desires. It was as though she had not been allowed to use her own mind until Albert was gone. She understood that he intended the best for her, but in managing her career and being her partner, he had taken independence from her the same way that her family and then the New York ballet scene had directed her every move. In many ways they had been hollow years, filled with bright lights, costumes, rehearsals, applause, and loneliness. She truly had been his marionette.

Dining at a restaurant a few miles out of Salt Hill Bay was uneventful yet fulfilling. They easily conversed about Shane's work, Annie's garden prospects for the coming season, her interest in repainting her living room walls. The conversations were light, comfortable, as well as warmly companionable.

When Annie turned her head toward where an elderly man played a piano, Shane's eyes caressed her slender neck and beautiful face. The impulse to touch her was strong, but he knew this could be entirely the wrong move for Annie. He couldn't help but wonder what she was thinking. Her life with a man had been over for a few years. Had she given up on ever loving someone again?

When she turned and looked back at Shane, her eyes met his and they were both caught in an unforeseen moment.

Shane smiled to mask his own emotions. "Care to dance?" he asked as he began to stand.

Annie felt a wave of fear as she looked up at him. "Oh, I think I've had enough dancing to last a lifetime," she said with an attempt at humor.

"Not with me," he said as he extended his hand. "Come on, Annie, there are other couples out on the dance floor – let's go."

Her hesitation was noticeable but she stood, placed her hand in his, and walked with him closer to the piano and other couples dancing. The move close to him, into his arms, was never where Annie thought to be. He held her close; his body warm and confident. They were silent as the pianist went through five pieces before he lingered long enough for the dancers to disperse. At that point, Annie declared that she needed some water and they returned to their table.

Having enjoyed a nightcap at the restaurant when the evening ended, Shane drove to Annie's home and parked the car. As she started to thank him and placed her hand on the car's door, he reached over and took her left hand in his for just a moment.

"Don't go," he said.

Those two words left Annie feeling paralyzed.

She looked at him with questions in her eyes. "Did you want to come in?"

"I do, but I might not leave."

Annie felt her throat grow dry and the adrenalin rush in her abdomen was strong. This was what she had both yearned for and feared. She didn't know what to do or say. She looked down at her hands, now clasped together in her lap, then she looked up at the lights on the street. "I can't," she said, and then she was gone.

Shane rested his head back on the car's seat and closed his eyes. When he opened them and looked toward her house, the door was closed and the lights were out. After just moments, he maneuvered the car toward his apartment, a deep, heavy feeling inside.

Annie sank down to her knees in the darkness of her home, Daisy brushing against her as if to ask what was wrong. With her slim fingers covering her face, Annie lowered her forehead to the carpet and cried. *What is this? What have I done?*

Shane drove mindlessly through town, analyzing the relationship he treasured. Annie had drawn his attention before he could clearly see her face that morning when they first met. He loved her before he ever said a word to her; *love at first sight.*

Part of him wanted to go back to that dark cottage, pound on her door and ask why. What was amiss between them? Was she placing too much importance on the years between them? Or was it Albert? The man had been handsome, wealthy, charming. Shane questioned what her reasoning might be.

When morning came, neither called the other to coordinate their walk. By nine, Annie sank into a chair and curled up in a fetal position. It would be one of the few times in more than three years that she had not walked the town or the beach.

In his apartment, Shane drank hot coffee and stared at his computer. He didn't feel like working, and yet the expectation was there from his employer. His fingers sought the keys as he once again was drawn to the photos of Annasheeva. *Annie.* How was he going to go on without the possibility of her in his life?

When darkness took over the house and then the town, Annie moved to turn lights on in her living room and kitchen. She fed Daisy then went to her room and sat on the edge of her bed. She lay back against the pillows, her eyes to the ceiling. After silent and still moments there, she moved her legs to the side, her feet to the floor and stood. She went to the hall closet and slipped her arms into a jacket then locked and left the house.

She walked through town, her eyes focused on her feet, looking up occasionally. She hadn't eaten all day – she didn't want to. She didn't know what she wanted to do. With her hands tucked into deep pockets, she made a turn, crossed the street, and walked back to her cottage.

Shane had not left his apartment all day. The chilled early spring temperatures and dampness in the air did not draw him out, and the thought of walking alone was more than he could handle. His every thought when not working was about Annie. He missed her to the extent that he, too, had not consumed more than his coffee and a bite from a slice of burnt toast.

Returning to her cottage, Annie hung her coat in the closet and then turned lights off. She went to her bed and lay across it, pulling a quilt over her legs. The painful pit in her stomach was not from lack of food. It was a different nourishment she required, one which would fill her heart. Everything hurt.

She resented the years separating Shane from her; she recalled what she was doing in those seventeen years before he was born. In a sense, she understood that she also had not been born. Her life had not belonged to her, but to her choreographers and the audiences who came expecting precise, graceful movements, earned by intense practice.

This hurtful experience was new to her; she had no thought for what to do. Life had been a matter of accepting what came: her career as a dancer, her role as Albert's wife. What was this about having a choice and making the wrong one? Annie pulled the quilt closer to her chest, curled up on her side, and fell asleep.

Shane took a sip from coffee he'd heated, threw on a jacket, and left his apartment. He walked toward the sea then veered away and walked through town. It was an exercise in movement, nothing more. With every step his thoughts were of Annie. He couldn't get the vision of her out of his mind. He loved the way she seemed to glide through her small home, taking care of it and her cat. She had been famous, known around the world, and yet here she was in a small New England town living the most simple of lives. He couldn't help but wonder if she was lonely for her husband.

He knew her well enough to know that she did not miss dancing and the city which had been her home. And he wondered, too, what kept her from allowing them to both be happy in one another.

To Shane, in many respects, Annie seemed more youthful than he, and her looks were undeniably outstanding. He stopped in front of their place to have coffee – it was closed. He wanted to walk to her cottage and knock on her door. He instead reversed his direction and walked back to his apartment.

Two days later, Shane shrugged on a light jacket and left his apartment. He walked toward the coffee aroma he detected a block away and, when he reached the café, he hesitated and then walked on. Minutes later he was standing at Annie's front door knocking lightly.

Wearing a pale pink shirt and jeans, she opened the door. She looked about twelve. They stared at one another for what seemed an eternity.

"Annie," he said, "let's not do this anymore. This staying apart is senseless and, besides that, it's killing me."

The tears formed in her eyes and she quickly wiped them away.

"Want some coffee?" she asked.

Shane's reply was to step inside and then he saw Daisy and reached down to give her several long strokes. The cat wound her way around his ankles so that he couldn't safely take a step. Annie and Shane looked at one another and laughed before Shane picked up the cat and spoke softly to her as he followed Annie to the kitchen.

They sat at her small table, Daisy making herself comfortable on Shane's lap as Annie poured two steaming cups of coffee.

"Have you been walking?" he asked.

"A bit, not so much," she said as she glanced in his eyes. "And you?"

"Not so much," he said. "It about made me sick to

think of going near the beach without you at my side. Annie, what happened to us?"

She held back the tears as she thought, as she knew, they'd fallen in love.

"Maybe we got too close," she said.

Shane looked at her and shook his head in denial. "I don't think getting 'too close', as you put it, is the problem. I think admitting it might be hard for you, Annie. It's not hard for me. It feels right to me, like second nature. I've missed you so much I felt like I was dying."

The tears formed in her eyes and spilled onto her pretty face.

Daisy knowingly jumped down to the floor and Shane moved toward Annie, placing his square hands on her shoulders. "I've been holding back from saying what I feel. I know it's hard for you; it's not hard for me at all. What is it in your head that is keeping us apart?"

Annie wiped her tears away and looked at him. "Shane, I'm forty-nine years old. You're a young man. What are you? Thirty? Thirty-one?"

"Thirty-two."

"That's seventeen years, Shane. I'm old enough to be your mother. It wouldn't work."

"Annie, do you think I care about seventeen years? No one, no one in the world, has ever drawn me in as you have. I'd be dead without you, Annie. I was physically and mentally a wreck when I met you. You made me mend; you helped me in every way to grow stronger. And it's not because I'm grateful, although I am; it's because I am one-hundred percent crazy about you. You, Annie, you."

Annie stood and took her half-full cup to the sink. "I can't, Shane. It's just not right."

"What's not right? When is love not right, Annie?"

"Shane," she said turning to face him, "I could never give you children. You're a young man with a wonderful future. You should have your own family."

Shane closed his eyes for a moment and then opened them and looked at her. "Annie, it was never my goal in life to produce children. Sure, I like kids and I'm pretty sure I'd enjoy one or two, but what I want is to share a life with someone I love. That would be you."

"And in twenty years, I'll be nearly seventy, Shane – are you really thinking a woman that age would appeal to you? No. I can't do that. I can't."

Shane threaded his fingers through thick hair and closed his eyes. Then he opened them again and looked at her. "What then? Are you giving up on me, Annie? Did you give me back my life to turn away from me?"

Annie placed her hands over her face as tears flowed and she shook her head from side to side. "I've loved what we had," she said as she blotted the moisture away with a napkin. "My hope is for a continued friendship."

Shane was quiet as he studied the face of the woman he loved. "Okay. We'll be friends, because I don't want an existence without you. Do you understand that, Annie? We'll go for our walks and we'll have coffee and occasional meals together, and we'll haunt some antique shops for things we both like, but we're not going to put time between us again."

She nodded and said nothing.

"Would you like to go for a walk now? It's pretty nice outside. Spring is here. Our beach will be calling us home soon, and for now we can walk the town, stop for coffee."

"We just had coffee," she said.

"We'll have more," he replied. "Come on, grab a

jacket; let's go."

For weeks, into late June, they walked, stopped for coffee, dined together at least twice each week, and stole occasional days for antiquing. Every moment together was treasured by both. They'd known one another for a full year.

It was a beautiful day with full sun shining and profusely blooming flowers loving the sea air. Shane met Annie at the shore, taking her hand as she moved carefully across the rocks before removing her sandals. They walked in unison, enjoying the call of the gulls and the crisp morning air until they reached their rock. Once there, Shane looked to the sea and then to Annie.

"I have something I need to tell you," he said.

Annie felt a chill and could tell by his expression that this wasn't going to be easy for either of them.

"The company I work for wants me in New Mexico."

Annie could not believe what she heard.

"Do you mean for a business trip?"

Shane looked at her and then at his feet before he looked back toward the sea. "They want me to relocate."

Annie could not fathom why she was hearing this horrific statement; certainly it couldn't be real. She was silent.

"Annie, it may only be for a year, but the projects I'm working on need some trouble-shooting and that's a major reason they hired me, for trouble-shooting. I may end up traveling to New York occasionally, but basically they'd like me in New Mexico for the next year or two."

Annie felt her heart sink. The shock and pain was unbearable. "I see."

Shane rubbed his face and the slight stubble on his chin from not having shaved that morning. He loved her. He loved her ferociously, as he had never loved before, but Annie was inaccessible. It was becoming more about the agony and longing than he could have imagined.

"I need to close up my place, get furnishings packed and moved. I can't believe I'm leaving Salt Hill – I love it here."

"When will you go?" Annie managed to ask in a steady voice.

"In two weeks. They'd like me there for early July. I'll stay here for the fourth. Can't think about how much I enjoyed last year, the fireworks, the joyfulness of the holiday and this town. It sure wouldn't be the same celebration in New Mexico."

As they turned to walk back to town for their morning coffee, Annie made an excuse for going home instead. This was the most distressing time in her life. The fear she'd felt all along was coming to fruition. Shane was leaving.

Chapter Ten

Two days after Independence Day, with a memorable fireworks display bursting color over the harbor, Shane was gone. His departure from Salt Hill Bay was ghostly, as if he might have been an apparition – someone intangible.

Annie felt numb. They had dinner together at her cottage the night before, Shane ending the evening by lifting Daisy into his arms to say farewell. Annie had all she could do not to lose the contents of her stomach and to not sob.

When morning came, it was quiet. Shane left without a last time to see Annie; Annie curled onto her side across her bed. The tears wouldn't come. She was certain that if they did, they would not stop. Everything felt dark and empty. How was she to go on without even a glimpse of Shane on the shore, in the café, at her cottage, in her heart? As conflicted as she was about this love, she had no good idea what to do about it. He'd expressed his feelings. She'd pushed him away.

Three weeks after his departure, Annie found a colorful postcard from New Mexico in her mail slot. Without reading the back, she held the card to her chest, closed her eyes, and felt warm tears streaming onto her face. She wiped them away and turned the card to read the message. A small label reflected his new address.

Hi Annie and Daisy, It's colorful everywhere you look here, I think you'd like it. I miss you both terribly. Shane.

Annie read the words and read them again. In the living room, she propped the card up where she could see it from her chair. When she went to the kitchen for tea, she took it with her. When she walked later that day, she placed the postcard in the pocket of her long skirt.

Walking the shoreline was something she now did exclusively to sooth her ankles. The call of the gulls, the glorious sunrises and sunsets, none of that mattered. Annie's thoughts were always the same. She would not look up and see Shane waiting for her, and she would not look in the direction of their rock. What once had been a seductive pleasure, tortured feet relaxed in salty swirl, was now only a daily task. Some days she walked once, not feeling strong enough to leave the cottage twice. At summer's end, Annie had collected four postcards from Shane and had sent him one from Salt Hill Bay. Afraid to write something revealing, she noted that Daisy missed him and hoped he was well.

Every moment of every day was a challenge – Annie did not know herself well enough to comprehend what she felt. Decisions of the heart had not previously been hers to make; it was simpler that way.

When a phone call came early one morning, Annie picked up her phone thinking it would be a telemarketer. Shane's voice came through as if she'd been struck by lightning.

"Annie, wow, so good to hear your voice. How are you? How's my Daisy?"

Annie felt her mouth go dry as her heart pounded. "Shane, Daisy and I are okay. Is everything all right?"

Shane laughed. "Yes, everything is okay. The job is demanding; I go into the office about three days a week.

I'm renting a small house. When I'm home, I work about fifteen hours each day. I like the work but I miss our walks on the beach. Have you been walking each day?"

Annie moved to sit down. "Yes, I walk. Do you?"

She could hear Shane sigh. "Not regularly. So, how's Daisy doing?"

"She's okay; slowing down a bit I think."

He was silent for a few moments. "I can't describe how much I miss you, that cat, and Salt Hill. It's pretty here, Annie, lots of artists around, but nothing like Salt Hill. It must be getting cold there now."

Annie closed her eyes and then opened them as Daisy jumped up and onto the arm of her chair. "Yes, autumn has arrived. The trees are pretty with their reds and golds; there's a definite chill in the air."

"We never went apple-picking," he said reflectively. "We should have done that."

Annie thought about what he'd said, as if their only chance to pick apples was gone forever.

"Annie, you there?"

"I'm here." She brushed tears away and stroked Daisy.

"I miss you, but I guess I said that, didn't I? I wouldn't have left, Annie. You know I wouldn't have taken this move if things were different."

Annie swallowed back tears. "Well, the warmer climate is probably best for you right now. You've had extensive surgery; your body must enjoy the Southwestern warmth."

Shane was silent.

They were both silent, clinging to their phones and the connection to one another.

"Are you going out for your walk this morning? It's pretty early here, five-fifteen. I wanted to catch you before you head out."

"Yes, I'll be going soon." She wanted to add that it was a struggle without him. She wanted to tell him that she loved him and she wanted him to come back, even if just to walk at his side, to sit across from him for coffee, to browse for antiques. She didn't.

When their call ended, Annie held the phone and looked at it, as if she could see into it. She pulled her legs up under her, put her head back on the chair, and closed her eyes. No, she would not walk – not then. She barely felt enough energy to get up and move about her home.

The truth was that sadness had become normal. Annie expected to wake up each day feeling as though her heart had broken; her stomach rejected food, her feet and ankles ached. This business of being caught up in an unmanageable love was torture: sad, screaming, mutilating torture. It was new. She never felt this before, even after she lost Albert.

She recalled her married life. That existence had been filled with dance, music, expectations of performance at every level. There had been brief moments in her life when Annie wondered if everyone lived this way, an arranged day, hour, minute. All orchestrated to present a circle of completeness, but was it? She had thoughts of children; Albert did not. He never said why. He simply smiled, patted her hand, and changed the subject. She had believed that she was happy, with Albert and her career, but now she wasn't so sure.

Annie sank further into her chair, clasping the phone to her heart. She became critical of herself for questioning her relationship with Albert. He'd made the decision to leave his family in Europe, never to see them again. She suspected he held disdain for some, if not all, of his family. He sent them sums of money through a bank account. Parts of his life were private – no one had a need to know, not even his beloved Annasheeva.

Becoming his bride, Annie felt cherished. She understood that the audience's attraction to her was superficial. Albert nurtured her when she felt alone and lost in a world of bright lights and fame she sought to disguise. All those years with him she never questioned his decisions until now. Had he been protecting his young wife or had he been taking his control to another dimension?

Before his death, he had spoken of her remaining in New York in their home, an assumption he'd made without ever a discussion. She had given it little thought until after he was gone and found herself living a life Albert had chosen. After a few days of visiting Salt Hill Bay, her decision was made. Friends were shocked to see her leave an elegant home and the most exciting city in the world, but, for the first time in her life, she hadn't cared what anyone else wanted or thought.

Annie had run from New York with no comprehension from what or to where – it felt right to leave that life behind. And now Shane ran. She replayed his words to her: he wouldn't have gone if things had been different. She understood.

Leaving the phone on a small table, she walked to the kitchen and made hot tea. She felt chilled with the colder weather and the stringent absence of the one she loved. She could admit that this dire feeling was due to what she longed for most, being with Shane Bellows. And even professing this to herself, Annie felt a sense of shame in the yearning.

Walking in town the next day, Annie saw displays of pumpkins being replaced with Christmas decorations of all kinds – advertisements regarding holiday sales dotted the store windows. She stopped in front of the café where she thought she might have coffee for the first time since Shane's departure, but then she turned around and walked home. The thought of Christmas without Shane was misery. She would not put up a tree. She would have no one for whom to buy a gift. She would buy fresh catnip and a piece of haddock for Daisy.

On Christmas Eve the phone rang and Annie knew whose voice she would hear.

"Hi, Annie. I called to wish you and Daisy a wonderful Christmas. What are your plans?"

Annie held her breath for a moment. "Oh, the usual. A festive little dinner for Daisy and me. How about you?"

Shane's response was soft and subtle. "Friends invited me over. I'm heading there this evening for a buffet and again tomorrow for dinner." There was a brief hesitation. "It won't be as nice as last year. I loved our tree, everything. I miss you, Annie."

Annie's tears flowed freely. She said nothing and then she heard him say, "Well, I'll let you go. I just wanted to touch base. Merry Christmas, Annie, and Daisy too."

Annie listened, unable to speak, and then she heard the soft click disconnecting them. She closed her phone and sobbed.

Months went by with no word from Shane. Annie resolved to live without him, to deny herself any feelings. He was young and handsome; she did not expect him to travel life alone. She imagined him with other women, or one woman, and she envisioned him dancing as sometimes he did with her and Daisy, teasing with his suave moves to a lively tempo. Of course, she thought, he would not stay in his rental and work – his world was expanded to making friends and meeting new people. His life, everyone's, was meant to be lived with enthusiasm and joy. She wanted that for him, and she wanted it for herself. Somehow she'd missed the merriment of dating, being young. It had all been stolen away from her by the stage lights.

When summer came to Salt Hill Bay, Annie resolved to once again walk the shores to soothe her aching limbs. The first time she slipped her sandals off and maneuvered the rocks before the sand, she thought of Shane, how he took her hand so often. She knew it was necessary to think of something else – she needed to walk and she needed to concentrate on what she would do with her sedate life.

After the first few days of walking alone as she had before Shane, Annie went to the café for coffee. A woman behind the counter commented that she hadn't seen her in a while, as if it had only been a few weeks since Annie was last there. Annie smiled, paid for her coffee, and walked home. She sat down on her front porch and picked up the small town paper. An article on the front cover caught her eye – a local battered women's shelter was in its fifth year and needed volunteers. Annie thought about the possibility briefly then made the call. She would give them six hours twice weekly – training would begin in four days.

Walking into the old brick structure for her first day of training, Annie wore an ankle length grey skirt and a navy blue shirt. Other than dancing, this would be her first instruction in something for which she had no knowledge. The women at the front desk seemed surprised to see Annie – her delicate features, graceful steps, and flowing clothing. They welcomed and liked her immediately. When asked if she had any special skills or interests, she told them she knew ballet; they suggested that she might offer to teach a few steps to some of the women. It could be fun, they advised.

It became a ritual. She helped to serve lunch, sort donated clothing, and then at two she pressed the CD player, eliciting soft classical music for basic steps. No one suspected that she had been a famous dancer.

Annie became a favorite among the shattered lives. She taught those who cared to learn, including a handful of young children, how to use their arms, their shoulders, their necks, to enhance the balance and movement of their legs.

One evening, after having walked the shores as well as fulfilled her time at the shelter, Annie took a warm shower and slipped into bed. She called to Daisy to join her. When the cat didn't comply, Annie went to look for her and found her curled up on what had been Shane's bed. Annie watched her, her breathing steady and slow, before she moved out of the room and into her own. When morning came and Daisy wasn't there to complain about not having her breakfast, Annie went again to Shane's old room. Daisy was there, still.

Annie stroked the soft fur and dripped warm tears onto the old cat. She leaned onto the bed, wrapping her arms around Daisy, telling her what a wonderful friend she had been and how much she would miss her.

Later that day, she wrapped Daisy in her favorite blanket, placed her in a small old leather suitcase, and dug a grave in the garden. Every shovel of soft earth brought tears.

With the grave complete and the suitcase settled into the ground, Annie covered it and then arranged shells and stones in the form of a heart. She sat on the ground by the grave and cried. She wanted to share this with Shane, but she had not heard from him in months. He had his life to lead. And what could he do anyway? This was her sadness; she had no place to put the grief other than in her own heart. She would miss Daisy terribly.

The following week, while Annie was volunteering, an eight year-old girl named Bella watched as Annie danced with five women of all ages. Bella noted the way Annie's feet moved in exact rhythm with the music.

"Were you always a dancer?" the dark-haired child asked as Annie slipped her feet into walking shoes.

Annie was stunned – no one else had ever asked. "Not always," she said, "but I do like to dance. What about you? Do you like to dance?"

The child's answer was tentative, non-committal. Annie offered to teach her some first steps. Bella didn't accept, but she didn't refuse. The next time Annie danced with the women in her group, Bella moved forward and tried some of the graceful arm and toe moves. Annie watched and remembered, certain that this little girl could be trained. She had a natural flow to her arms and the core of her body swayed to accommodate balance and timing.

Three weeks after noting Bella's prowess, Annie walked into the shelter to discover that Bella and her mother had gone. Annie felt a deep sense of loss for herself and for the child. She could have given her enough dance instruction to keep her interested for life, or at least to keep as a joyful memory.

Chapter Eleven

One year after Daisy's death, Annie went out into the garden after dark with a little votive. She placed it on the grave and struck a match to start the flame's glow. She sat down on the warm ground and watched the flickering light, tears welling in her eyes for the losses she'd endured: Albert, Shane, Daisy, Bella. After more than an hour sitting in the dark, surrounded with summer's end flowers and the sound of crickets, Annie decided that she needed another pet; she would see about a cat or a small dog. A few days later she took a taxi to a shelter one mile out of town and came home with a large dog two years old. He'd been the companion to an elderly man who had passed away. Sherlock; his name suited him as he checked out and snooped into everything in Annie's cottage. Then he took her favorite chair as his own. Annie smiled.

Not a day passed when Annie didn't think of Shane. Sometimes she wondered about Bella or mused about how Daisy would have bossed Sherlock around. Occasionally she would think about Albert, commanding the orchestra or entertaining in their home. But, no matter how she tried, her thoughts returned to the man she hadn't allowed herself to fully possess, the man she hadn't allowed to fully possess her.

With Sherlock tethered via a strong leash, Annie often found herself pulled along the shoreline and throughout the town. People smiled seeing Annie's slight form being tugged by a dog larger in mass than his companion.

She worked at training him not to surge ahead, to stop when she told him to, and to sit as told. He became her lifeline, something to care for, a reason to exist. The dog seemed to be a combination of breeds; he was beige, almost a creamy white, with a slight curl to the coat on his large frame. Annie thought of him as a Great Dane Poodle with soulful amber eyes.

It took no time at all before Sherlock was making himself comfortable on two thirds of Annie's bed.

He was a place to put her love, a gift for her tattered heart. Watching him sniff at the familiar places Daisy had frequented, Annie explained to the sweet dog that once there was Daisy, whom she loved as she would now love him. Before long, she had begun to call him 'Lock-star' as she ruffled his floppy ears; they were dedicated friends.

Weeks and seasons went by without a word from Shane. Annie missed him more than she thought capable of; she hoped for his good health and happiness. She had elected not to have him complete her life; he had wisely moved on.

She continued to work at the shelter twice weekly and her walks with Sherlock became the light of her days. She thought about Daisy, the little cat patiently waiting for her to come home each time the shore or town had beckoned. Having a dog at her side was comforting and companionable – something to concentrate on other than her memories. *When will I cease to miss him? When does this deep ache for him subside?*

Routine became necessary with Sherlock's need to go

out and his pure love of exploring the town's offerings. While there were times during winter when Annie might have elected to stay home, Sherlock was ready to go.

"Really, Lock-star? It's cold out there; let's stay home."

The dog cocked his head to one side and looked at her with *please* in his eyes. They went out to walk, Annie often feeling tired but willing for Sherlock's sake.

Annie began to think that something within her body might be wrong. She waited out the ill feeling, hoping it would go away. Other than an occasional podiatrist for her feet, there had been no doctor necessary before in her life. New York was filled with the finest, but Annie was never sick. Since arriving in Salt Hill Bay, she had not required any physical assistance. She began to think that she might need to see someone; her abdomen didn't feel right.

At the shelter, a doctor, a woman who Annie guessed to be similar to her in age, came once each week to tend to the inhabitants. Annie took her aside one day and told her the symptoms. She was advised to have an ultrasound where the doctor practiced nearby.

Annie waited another couple of weeks before making an appointment. It didn't take long to determine that Annie had a liver condition which was creating havoc with her digestive system. She needed medication and she needed food. Annie had not been eating well and she'd been taking more over-the-counter pain relief than was recommended on the medication's label.

Often feeling tired, she walked Sherlock for small increments of time and felt bad cheating him out of his beloved walks on the shore. Her illness, she was told, could be serious and, if nothing else, would take time to restore the liver to good health.

102

Three years after her diagnosis, Annie felt wilted. She endeavored to take good care of Sherlock – his feedings were simple while his longing for walks was not so easy. With summer approaching, Annie decided that she would push to walk once again at the shore where Sherlock's eyes glistened with excitement to see other dogs and to walk in the emerging surf. She smiled at his antics and felt thankful for having such a wonderful creature in her life.

On her third morning at the sea, her feet enjoying the soothing salt wash, Sherlock prancing in the shallow incoming tide, Annie looked to the sea and then straight ahead. She stopped. She could not believe what seemed to be a mirage, and then he walked up to her, hands tucked into jean pockets. They stood just inches apart. He had no smiles, no words, until Annie took a deep breath, reminding her that she was now sixty to his forty-three years.

With only silence between them, Sherlock came running to Annie's side and she reached down to clip his leash onto his collar. When she looked back at Shane, she still wasn't sure she was seeing him.

"Annie," he said, "looks like you have the dog I always thought I'd have." He reached down and gave the large creature several good pats and then he stared at Annie's beautiful face.

"Don't chase me away again," he said, and then they were in one another's arms.

When Annie pushed away enough to look at his face, more handsome than ever, he saw her tears and she noted his. His hands went to her face, his thumbs pushed the moisture aside. He kissed her and then they were molded together again.

"I can't believe this," Annie said.

He gave her a firm squeeze then turned his attention again to the dog. "What's this guy's name?"

"Sherlock; he came with the name."

"He's great. What is he?" Shane asked while rubbing the dog's ears.

"A dog," Annie said, and they laughed and walked back toward the shore.

Once away from the rolling tide, they stopped. "I'm shocked, thrilled to see you. But still shocked," Annie said facing him.

"I know. It was probably unfair of me to surprise you. I called the café and talked to our buddies there. They told me you didn't come in anymore but that they saw you walking past. I knew you were still here. I didn't tell you I was coming because I was afraid you'd tell me not to."

Annie shook her head and tugged lightly at Sherlock's leash as they began to walk. They were silent for long moments, each with their own thoughts. Shane looked out to the sea, squinting into morning sun. Annie looked at his mature, handsome face. Years of sun and time had etched little lines at the corners of his eyes.

He observed her catching a long glance at him, then noticed the shell earrings adorning her ears. He smiled, happy that his gift endured, even in his absence. "Let's go for a coffee."

"Sherlock can't go into the café, and I won't leave him tied outside. We could go to my place."

Shane nodded. "That sounds great. How's Daisy doing?"

Annie wore a faint smile but tears filled her eyes.

Shane stopped as he placed his hands on her shoulders. "Is she gone?"

Annie allowed the tears to fall. "Yes, several years

ago. She was ancient, you know. She's in my garden."

"Are you hoping to grow her again?" he asked in an attempt to make light of the situation. When he saw her tears mixed with the smile, he stopped to take her in his arms. "Annie, that was a very bad attempt to make a joke. I know you loved that little cat and I did too. I don't know how I left here. I had strong attachments; it was a tough decision. I was hoping, you know, that when I told you I was going, you'd beg me to stay. I wanted to stay. I wanted to, Annie."

Annie stiffened her shoulders against the memory of loss, Shane and then Daisy – it had been almost unbearable. As he held her closer, Annie's shoulders sank into him and, for the first time in years, possibly in her life, she felt she belonged.

Shane's hold on her was more than physical. His hands on her slim back felt right. He pressed the right side of his face to the right of hers, closed his eyes, then opened them as he moved her just inches away. "We need to talk."

Annie stiffened enough to brush tears away and glance to the sea before finding herself mesmerized by his gray eyes. "Let's go make some coffee," she said as they turned to walk, Sherlock leading the way.

At the path to her cottage they stopped, Shane's hand wrapped around Annie's. He looked at the small house, so filled with memories of a time when he needed care. The woman he loved saw him through and now he wondered how he'd ever left this place.

"I was here last night," he said.

Annie looked at him with surprise. "You were?"

He nodded. "I stood here about ten o'clock. I saw a few lights on here and there – I was hoping to catch a glimpse of you."

"Why didn't you knock on the door?"

Shane smiled and looked down at his feet then back up into Annie's sweet face. "I wanted to see you again exactly the way we met years ago, on the beach."

Annie thought that if she didn't change the subject, tears would find their way to her eyes again. "Let's go in and make that coffee," she said as she let go of his hand and walked with the key ready to open the door.

Inside Shane hesitated as his eyes scanned the familiar room.

Annie unclipped the leash from Sherlock; the dog shook then jumped into what was now his chair.

Shane laughed as he followed Annie to the kitchen.

Annie made coffee then turned to look at Shane who had seated himself at the kitchen table. She thought about how this must be a dream. Before Shane, everything about her life had order. After Shane, everything she did, everywhere she went, every thought she had, seemed connected to his memory. She wanted desperately to get over him, and yet she wanted never to forget what she felt for him.

Annie placed a cup of coffee before him then poured one for herself and sat down.

"Annie," he said, placing the cup down after finding the brew too hot to swallow, "what would you say to me moving in with you?"

Annie gulped and wondered if she could find speech. After several moments of Shane's intense eyes upon her, she looked at him. "Why would you do such a thing?"

Shane had no hesitation. "Because when I was having a hard time with my injuries and then the surgeries, we lived here for months in total unison. I never felt more at home, more at ease in my life. I want to be with you, Annie."

Annie shook her head and looked away.

"Annie," he persisted, "it's the age thing, I know. We're seventeen years apart. Your husband was fifteen years older than you. Why is an additional two years significant? It's not, Annie. Give us a chance. If nothing else, I think we could enjoy a life together – we've done that; it worked."

"But you had a nice apartment, you liked your space and all your copper pieces collected on our antique excursions."

"I still have them, Annie. I left a lot in New Mexico, but I brought my copper. I could decorate my room, or maybe we could have them around the house. The lanterns are nice; I could see one at your hearth."

Annie looked at him and asked the question prominent on her mind. "What else did you leave in New Mexico?"

Shane understood her meaning. He took a sip of coffee then held the warm cup in his hands. "Okay, I guess it's time to fill in the gaps. I did have a relationship. She was great in many ways. I was with her for more than five years and then she asked if we were going to get serious, meaning married. I told her probably not. She wasn't happy and wanted to know why. I told her I didn't feel what I should to get married. It wouldn't be fair to be with her when my heart was with another."

Annie looked away and then back at him.

"You," he said, "if you have any doubts about who I'm talking about, it's you, Annie."

"Shane…"

"I know, those seventeen years again. They don't matter, Annie. You're thinner than when I left here and I'm concerned about why, but otherwise you look the same. I want us to try; if you're so against it, I won't push. I'll get another apartment, maybe eventually a house. I wish you'd give it a chance. I promise to keep my distance if that's what you require – I'll be an excellent housemate. I'll vacuum, I'll cook, I'll take Sherlock for walks when it's cold and you'd like to stay home. I won't try to sneak into your bed, I promise. I'll wait for an invitation."

Annie's lips spread into a smile and then into a laugh. "I don't know what to do with you," she said.

"I'll teach you," he responded.

Annie could feel her face flush as she looked away again. Her life with Albert was the only one sexually involved. He had been the instigator of all activity in their bedroom, formal in his pursuit while gentle and thoughtful. Annie suspected that there was much she didn't know regarding sex; it had not occurred to her that Shane would find an interest in her for an intimate relationship. She was not prepared to foster those thoughts.

"I don't know, Shane; you're what, forty-three? Was your love interest in New Mexico an older woman?"

Shane smiled. "She was five years younger than me."

Annie squirmed in her chair. "And that's the age you should be pursuing in a woman."

"Who made that rule?"

Annie sighed as quietly as she could. "If you need a place to stay until you figure things out, you may stay here. I think you should consider looking for your own space. You loved your place – you made it welcoming. I'm not considering any other relationship with you than as a dear friend. If that's acceptable, then yes, you may move into the spare room."

Shane took a long swallow of coffee, placed the cup down, and looked at Annie. Her eyes were a luminous blue and her hair, the mix of blonde and silver, was softly styled, free-flowing, where he longed to place his hands. "Okay."

"How did you get here? Did you drive?"

"Yes, my car is parked in front of the café on Main Street. Everything I own, including my copper pieces, is packed into the trunk and back seat."

"No furniture?"

"No furniture. I left what I had for the new tenant. He was young and broke – I remember those days."

Annie finished her coffee and stood. "Would you like to go for your car so that you can get settled in?"

Shane stood and carried his cup to the kitchen sink. He reached out and tugged gently on Annie's hair then turned to the door, Sherlock following.

"Hey," he said to the dog, "did Daisy tell you I was easy?"

Annie called to Sherlock and the obedient creature sat. "He'll be fine here," she said to Shane, "but expect to grow a shadow. He's very social."

Shane smiled, gave the dog a pat on his head, and left.

Annie looked at the closed door. What had she done? She wasn't so sure that letting Shane into her home was a good idea, yet contemplating their relationship was sweet. She would dispel anything romantic, and then her thoughts returned to their kiss.

After settling himself into the room where he'd once spent more than three months, Shane walked into the kitchen wearing jersey pajama bottoms, bare feet, and a gray t-shirt. Annie glanced at his attire, not surprised since he'd practically lived in this relaxed type of clothing while recovering from surgery. Now it seemed slightly provocative.

"I made some fresh lemonade," Annie said. "Would

you care for some?"

Shane sat down. "I'd love some, and I need to talk with you about my share of paying the expenses. I intend to pull my weight around here, financially as well as with chores. Tell me what you need, Annie. Make me a list."

Annie poured two glasses of lemonade and sat down across from him. "I do have one concern. We didn't discuss your dating."

Shane smiled as he swallowed a few sips of the cold drink. "Let me guess, no women in the house."

Annie looked at him and then reached down to pat Sherlock who lay at her feet. When she looked up at Shane she nodded. "Well, I wouldn't like it much if you brought someone here."

There was a silence. "Annie, it won't happen. I hope some day you understand: I don't want anyone but you, and I'll take whatever of you you're willing to give me."

Changing from the awkward subject of female guests, Annie asked about Shane's work.

"I'm pretty much doing the same thing, at home and on my computer. I'll look for a small table soon; I'll need to set up a little office space in my room. We could go antiquing for one."

"Since you left," she said, "there's a new place out on Main Street. It's filled with multiple dealers. You might try there."

"Sounds good, but you have to come with me. We'll have a day looking around. Does Sherlock like being in a car? I wouldn't mind another Cape day."

Annie smiled. "The only time I was with him in a car was when I met him and brought him home from the shelter. I walk him to the vet for his shots."

Sherlock wandered over to rest his chin on Shane's knee.

"Yes, Sherlock, I'll take you in my car for our day trips, I promise."

The large dog half moaned his pleasure at being invited.

Shane laughed. "He's a great dog – I miss Daisy, but this guy has charisma too. I think we're going to be good friends."

They were quiet for a few moments as Shane rubbed Sherlock's ears and talked to the dog with soft murmurings. Then he looked at Annie. "Tell me what you've been doing for the past several years. Anyone in your life?"

"Do you mean a man?"

Shane shrugged. "Yeah, I guess so, or anyone new."

Annie leaned back in her chair. "I don't date. I volunteer two days each week in a women's shelter just around the corner. I help with sorting donated clothes and I have a few basic dance classes with moms and kids as students. It keeps me feeling limber and it's fun for the women and children."

Shane nodded. "That's pretty neat. No men in your life, Annie? Is there a reason for that?"

"I suppose so. I do fine on my own."

Shane gave her a quick smile. "Until now."

He wanted to ask about her health. Noticeably thin, still strikingly beautiful, her body was taught and spare. Shane feared she wasn't eating well.

"Are you okay, Annie? It looks like you've lost weight you didn't need to lose."

Annie took a deep breath. "I took a few more drugstore pain relievers than advised. I managed to annoy my system. I'm doing better." She closed that conversation by standing, washing her glass, and moving to the living room.

Shane watched her move – from the back, no one would be able to tell her frame from an active teen. He beckoned the dog to follow him as he walked into the living room and sat on the opposite end of the sofa from where Annie watched TV.

He glanced at her every few minutes, trying not to be conspicuous. Somehow, he thought, he needed to convince her that the years between them didn't matter. She was undoubtedly the most beautiful woman he had known, physically and emotionally. She was intelligent, sweet, and undeniably gorgeous. Years in New Mexico had not lessened his interest in her.

Chapter Twelve

With a desk and computer set up in his room, Shane disappeared most days after a walk on the beach and breakfast. Annie found him an easy companion. At noon he ventured out into the kitchen, most often to share sandwiches and fruit with Annie. Dinner was prepared together, unless it was Shane's famous pizza presented with a salad and a glass of red wine.

It was into the fourth week when Shane suggested they take Sherlock and ride to the Cape for lunch and antiques. Annie was thrilled; she had not wanted to suggest time away from his work.

"Where are we heading?" she asked, pulling a light sweater over her clothes.

"South," he answered. "Let's head out toward Barnstable, then maybe further on. What do you think?"

Annie smiled. "Let's go." She snapped the leash onto Sherlock's collar and took bottled water and a bowl for him. The dog danced with the idea of going out. In the car he watched the passing scenery as if it was the most beautiful sight he'd ever seen.

Annie and Shane commented on the quaint houses, the gentle landscape, and then began to find small shops welcoming them in to search for treasures. She watched and listened as Shane expressed his enthusiasm for the general area, never mentioning his time or the land in

New Mexico. Several years in another state, adjusting to that climate and certainly house styles unique to the Southwest, and yet it seemed not to have made an impression.

"Do you miss New Mexico?" she asked.

Shane smiled as he maneuvered the car through narrow Cape Cod roads. "No," he said with a quick glance to Annie. "It's a beautiful state with incredible mountains, but it didn't grab me. I like this, I like New England. The history of this place, the lay of the land, it's all appealing. I missed Salt Hill Bay and the Cape more the longer I was away." He thought about adding how much he'd missed Annie. He glanced at her but decided to wait. "I read books about this area while I was in New Mexico. Some of what I read dealt with the landscape and sea access, other books were of the rich history. I had empathy for the Founding Fathers – I learned a lot about lesser known heroes such as James Otis, Jr. He was a dynamo, a very influential guy who had a way with words as well as knowing his stuff. I always knew I'd be back here, and seeing you again was the icing on the cake. I can't believe how lucky I am to have found you."

Annie swallowed the emotion she felt and gave Shane a quick smile before she returned her eyes to the road.

At a weathered, barn-board antique shop, they pulled up close to the door, walked Sherlock for five minutes, then closed him into the car with his window down enough for him to enjoy the Cape air. Wistfully, he watched them enter the small building and disappear.

Inside Shane immediately found a large copper pitcher and then a smaller one in a similar style. Annie found a flow blue plate and then she looked through a tray of earrings. With aqua stones centered in gold circles, Annie placed one earring on and looked at it in a small mirror. She unfastened it and decided she would buy them. Shane walked close to her and took them from her hand. He held them to the light from a window and then closed his fingers around them as Annie watched.

"I'd like to get these for you," he said.

Annie stood motionless. She thought to protest but heard herself murmur a thank you as he placed the earrings with his intended purchases.

"Would you like to look further?" Shane asked.

Annie smiled. "I think I've gone around this place three times. I'm happy with my earrings and plate."

Shane smiled and reached for her hand as they walked to where they would pay. Annie tentatively placed her hand in his and walked by his side. They let go for the time it took to pay for their purchases, then Shane took Annie's hand again as they walked to the car, Sherlock watching every step as they moved toward him. They continued on to two more shops and lunch before turning toward home.

"Did we have fun or what?" Shane asked Annie with a smile as they drove north to Salt Hill Bay. "I can't believe my luck finding more great copper pieces. I think I'm becoming a serious collector."

Annie smiled at his enthusiasm. "The pieces you found today are especially nice. The tall pitcher is an appealing shape; graceful, yet masculine."

"And you found more in the blue and white, a cup and saucer, right?"

Annie nodded. "It looks like I'm becoming a collector of two things myself: flow blue china and earrings."

They smiled at one another as Shane turned left onto a highway twenty minutes from home.

Annie rested her head back against the car's seat and

watched the scenery.

Shane glanced over at her profile, noting the feathery, pale hair against her left cheek. He wanted to touch her, to take her hand, but he understood that he needed to move slowly with Annie.

"When we get back, I thought I'd heat up some soup to go with a nice grilled cheese sandwich. What do you think?" he asked.

Annie looked at him and smiled. "I think I'm getting spoiled. You didn't cook when you stayed with me before. This is nice."

"Ah, but you were in charge back then, and I didn't know how to boil water. Living on my own taught me to become self-sufficient. I don't do anything gourmet, but I can put a meal together."

Annie smiled again. "You've done well – I'm very willing to let you cook any time you wish. The soup and grilled cheese sound perfect – warm and delicious."

Shane kept his eyes on the road ahead, surprised at his depth of feeling for this woman. He had loved her from the beginning without even knowing her name. With every step toward her on the beach that first morning, he prayed silently that she wasn't married, that she wasn't attached. Like a sea nymph, her feet seemed to barely touch the sand. Now she was in his car less than two feet away, and he was living in her small home. He wondered how he had managed to come so close to magic.

When he allowed his eyes to stray from the road ahead for just a moment, he could see that Annie's eyes were closed. The day was folding away as he found himself wishing that he could share her bed. While he understood that might never happen, he was longing for the closeness. To lay stretched next to Annie, to embrace her through the night, was his greatest hope.

As though she'd read his mind, she opened her eyes and turned to look at him. She smiled and he returned the smile.

"Tired?" he asked.

Annie shook her head gently side to side. "Not really. Mellow, that's what I think I am, just feeling mellow. This was such a nice day, Shane. Thank you."

Before Shane could speak, Sherlock maneuvered himself so that his head was resting on the back of Annie's seat. Shane reached with his right hand to scratch the dog's chin.

"He's like having a really well-behaved kid," Shane said, and they laughed.

The closer they were to Salt Hill Bay, the more Annie shifted in her seat with the familiar feeling of awkwardness. They would be home, sharing a small house and a meal. Her feelings for him were becoming defined. She could imagine herself in his arms and, while she hadn't thought she'd ever share a bed with another man, the concept of being with Shane had crept into her psyche, her self-conscious struggling rapidly to sweep the temptation out, as futile as the waves' attempt to wash the sand from the shore. He'd developed a physical and emotional strength in his years away. She was convinced it would be the wrong move to allow him more than what they had, a strong but simple friendship. More could jeopardize everything. Sharing a space together was enough for Annie – she wondered, however, if it would it be enough for Shane.

The remainder of the ride home was without conversation. When they pulled up to the cottage, Shane emptied the car of their purchases. Annie and Sherlock wandered out back to the garden so that he could have some time to romp after being in the car most of the day.

117

Annie sat down at a small bistro table she had purchased and decorated with bits of broken pottery, rocks, and shells. As she sat pondering the future of their relationship, Shane appeared in the doorway and asked if they should eat there in the garden. Annie agreed. Shane soon brought out a tray with their meals, two glasses, and a pitcher of lemonade.

"It'll be warm enough to swim pretty soon," he remarked, swallowing the last of his sandwich. "Do you swim?"

Annie brushed a few crumbs from her lips and shook her head. "Would you believe I never learned?"

"You're kidding. You don't swim?"

"Never had the chance to learn. We had a shallow pond of water in the back yard when I was little, but the ducks and geese claimed it. I'd walk in the water sometimes. There was a soft mud bottom, not the greatest place to swim."

"No beach? You never went on vacation where there was a pool?"

Annie shook her head from side to side again. "No vacations. We had a farm, small, but still one that needed daily attention. We never went away."

Shane thought about that little girl and wished he'd known her as a child. She must have been lonely, like he was.

"I, too, grew up on a farm, remember?" he said with a wink. "But a bunch of us used to go to the river most days when the weather was warm enough. Do you want to learn to swim? I could teach you."

Annie smiled. "Thank you, but no. Maybe twenty years ago I'd have taken you up on the offer, but now I'm content with walking the shore. So, you enjoy swimming?"

Shane nodded. "Yes. We had a watering hole on our farm too. It was deep enough to dive into and swim to the other side, maybe five-hundred feet across. Sometimes a cow would wander in – it was pretty funny."

"Did you swim in New Mexico?"

"Yes, almost every day. The complex where I lived had a pool. It actually helped in my healing, made me stronger and more agile. I might swim here in the ocean once in a while, but I think our walks on the sand will be therapeutic enough. We'll see. I can always join a local Y if I want to swim regularly."

With Sherlock fed and walked and dishes washed, they settled into their own seats in the living room where Shane switched on TV. Annie balanced a hot cup of coffee and pulled one leg up under her body as she watched him surfing the channels, looking for something interesting.

"I give up," he said with a smile. "Any suggestions?"

Annie smiled. "A good book?"

Shane turned the TV's volume down and sat, one leg crossed over the other at the ankle. "Or we could talk."

Annie felt her stomach tighten, a natural instinct for a nervous dancer.

"I'm stuck back on that Connecticut farm where you grew up, or where you began to grow up. Did you like it there, Annie?"

"I loved it. It was beautiful there and I recognized that even as a child. I loved roaming the pastures and the woods – there were always wonderful things to discover."

"Why did you leave? I mean, I know it wasn't your idea, but you were what, eight? Who let you go?"

Annie started to turn away and then she looked at

Shane. "I was sent for dance lessons when I was about five. My family must have thought I should have lessons in something that would give me some discipline. At some point, the ballet teacher recognized that I learned easily and practiced frequently. After a while, it was decided I should go to New York."

Shane looked at her, that beautiful face suddenly saddened.

"Weren't you lonely for the farm and your family?"

Annie's eyes went to the cup in her hands and then to the silent TV. "Yes, I missed home."

Shane tried to imagine a little girl living with strangers in New York City. "Did you go home once in a while? How often did your family visit?"

"They didn't. I went home once in a while, maybe twice each year in the beginning. After I became a teen, I seldom went back. I didn't fit in there. I still loved the area, but some of my family seemed to resent that I was becoming known, that I arrived home with silk dresses and velvet coats. I didn't understand. To me, these were the clothes bought for me – I was still me under them."

Shane swallowed, feeling emotional for a young girl not made welcome in her own home.

"What about you?" she asked. "You were a farm kid too. Did it fit you back then?"

Shane shifted in his chair and then stood. "I'm going to grab a coffee before I answer. Can I get you a refill?"

Annie held her cup for him to see. "I still have half a cup, but thank you."

Shane walked to the kitchen, poured the hot brew into his cup, and returned to his seat across from Annie. "I don't think I ever fit in back there."

Annie felt stunned with this revelation. He'd told her when they first met that his injuries had prevented him from doing heavy work on the farm. He'd felt that he'd disappointed his father.

"I never told you: I had an older brother, Blake. He took to the farm, a real natural. When he was fourteen, he was killed jumping off a bridge into a river near the house. He'd done it a million times, but this time he hit his head. My parents were shattered. I was two years younger than Blake and I became a ghost. My sister was a baby, an unexpected baby, and I think it took all of my mother's energy to take care of her. My father couldn't even look at me. I felt like he resented every bite of food I put in my mouth, like he wished it had been me in that river. I stayed as long as I could. At nearly eighteen, I joined the service. After I got out, I went to school for computer science, then back in the service. The rest you know. I was injured enough that I nearly gave up, until you, Annie. You saved me."

Annie could feel the liquid forming in her eyes and she looked away before looking back at him.

"I'm sorry," she said.

Shane gave her a wry smile. "I'm okay. Lots of people have worse tales to tell."

Annie thought about his words then moved them to the back of her mind. What she understood was that his injuries were far deeper than he had admitted to in years past. His family had failed him; perhaps they hadn't chosen to, but fate had set the scene.

Shane used the remote to change channels until he found a sit-com, asking Annie if that would do. She nodded and smiled, feeling immensely sad for the boy who had not known love. She wanted to hug him close, to tell him that was over, that he could live for himself now, but could he? And what did she have to offer? She could not give him children; she could not give him a

121

promised length of time. She could not forget that she was sixty to his forty-three years.

With Sherlock resting his large frame against Shane's legs, Annie smiled at the dog's insistence in being attached to one of them at all times.

Shane glanced over at Annie and laughed. "This guy has no problem doling out his affection, does he? How did you happen to end up with a dog?"

Annie shrugged. "I suppose it had something to do with Daisy. I felt that finding another cat might seem like a betrayal to her. Sherlock was pretty persuasive in the shelter – I couldn't resist. Does it bother your legs to have him there? He can come sit by me."

"No," Shane was quick to respond. "He's great. I like having him close."

Shane reached down, scratched behind the dog's ears, then turned his attention to the TV.

Annie looked at each of them then rested her head back on the sofa. This life with Shane was more than she had ever imagined would be hers.

Chapter Thirteen

With warm mornings and even warmer afternoons, Shane worked at his computer early, a cup of coffee at his side. Only when he heard Annie moving about in the kitchen would he leave his desk to join her and Sherlock, who was always ready to go out.

As he watched her hold the door open one morning for Sherlock's return, he smiled at the interaction. Sherlock brushed against Annie's legs as he entered, causing her pale blue robe to open, revealing a slim thigh.

She turned and caught Shane's eyes on her legs and then her face, feeling herself blush with his interest.

She thought about saying something as she pulled her robe back in place, but instead she walked to the refrigerator for Sherlock's breakfast then poured herself a cup of coffee.

"Breakfast?" she asked Shane.

"Depends on who's cooking," he said as he eased himself into a chair at the table.

Annie met Shane's eyes. "I doubt Sherlock is going to prepare us anything we'd want. Would you like eggs this morning?"

"I have an idea," he said. "Let's take fried egg sandwiches and coffee to the beach – a breakfast picnic."

In twenty minutes, the threesome was ready to leave

the house. Annie thought about her strict menu as a dancer, always watching the carbs, drinking more water than all other beverages combined. Living in Salt Hill Bay was like being on vacation, and adding Shane to the mix was pure joy. She understood that he could go away again, or meet someone he'd find and care for other than her, but Annie decided that in this moment she would allow herself to quietly love him. He didn't have to know – he *couldn't* know; she wasn't prepared to take their relationship to another level.

After sitting on their rock with breakfast, sharing morsels of it with Sherlock and the gulls, they slid to the sand and walked. Annie moved close to the water, the incoming tide. At one point, a large wave swept in and caught the hem of her long skirt, the material circling her ankles. Shane laughed when he saw her trying to untangle her legs from Sherlock's leash. Before she knew what was happening, he scooped her up into his arms and twirled her around in the shallow water as Sherlock enjoyed the playfulness.

Annie held on, her right arm around Shane's neck, her left hand on his right bicep. She felt like she was flying until the reality of his lips on hers brought her to an ecstatic stillness. Understanding that it would probably be the right thing to pull away from him, she leaned in closer for a deeper, longer kiss like no other she had ever imagined.

When he finally allowed her feet to touch the sand away from the sea, he did not release her. She loosened her hands from his arm and neck, feeling embarrassed with her genuine display of affection.

"Now," he said, looking down at her beautiful face, "that wasn't so bad, was it?"

Annie looked down at Sherlock and took hold of his

leash. When she looked back up into Shane's eyes, she expected he'd drop his hands to his sides or into his pockets as he often did. He held onto her, one hand moving to pull strands of her pale hair from her eyes.

"I love you, Annie," he whispered, and then he said it again as if in competition with the wind. At that point, he dropped his hands from her shoulders but clasped his left hand possessively over her right as they walked.

Everything he knew about this woman was positive. Initially he'd been drawn to her by the lithe body gracefully moving along the water's edge. And then it was her stunning face, the purity of her eyes, the tentative smile. He loved her and could feel her pulse beating with his own, the hand he clasped not resistant. He knew that this woman was made of something he needed and wanted in his life. She was his energy. For several years he'd existed without her, wondering every morning as he rose what she was doing at that moment. Before bed each night, his last thought was of Annie – where was she? What was she doing? During vacant moments in the day, whispers of her crept into his heart and made him long for simply being near her.

Annie released restrictions that day, that very moment when Shane possessed her hand gently, not in capture, but in want. The kiss, the embrace, long denied, yet anticipated. She loved him. There was no doubt, and now she struggled again with those years between them.

"Shane," she said as they walked through her front door, "we need to talk."

Shane unhooked Sherlock's leash and hung it by the door then turned to Annie, this time with his hands tucked into the pockets of his jeans. He knew – she was going to remind him that this wasn't going to happen.

"Yes, Annie," he said, "I know what you're about to

say. Could we have a coffee first?"

Annie looked at him and sighed. "Yes, but you get it while I change out of this wet skirt."

She turned and moved toward her bedroom, returning to the living room where hot coffee waited and Sherlock contentedly chewed on a dog toy.

Shane was sitting, his eyes on hers as she placed herself at the end of the sofa. There was silence except for the dog's chewing.

Shane took a sip from his coffee; Annie did the same. She held the cup in both hands as if for support.

"This morning," she said, "all of that caught me off-guard. You must know that."

Shane took another swallow of coffee. "I've always known the time would come when I would move forward and you would step back. I'm not apologizing, Annie."

She looked at him expecting exactly that, an apology. She looked away, wordless.

He watched her for a moment then placed his cup down and leaned forward, his elbows resting on his knees. "Who are you, Annie?"

She looked at him and felt tears form in her eyes. She gave no answer and then he was worried that he had offended her with the question.

"Annie? Tell me. Because I think your whole life has been orchestrated for you; that you ran here to Salt Hill Bay to find out who you were, what you loved. Everyone's been telling you how to live every moment, until you escaped to the sea. Isn't that true, Annie? Have you had a life you wanted?"

Annie sat perfectly still, her eyes on the hearth, and then she looked at him. "I don't know what I am other than a dancer. My identity is unknown."

"That's not true," he said. "You might not have

discovered yourself fully at this point, but you had the determination to leave behind the life that was programmed for you – to come here and live a simple existence at the sea. You found this cottage and a little cat, and when you lost her, you had the courage to find this huge character of a dog. Annie, you're making strides toward finding yourself. Your life was created first by family who sent you to dance in New York. And then by choreographers who told you what to eat and how much. Even your husband controlled your friends, your clothing, plans for each day. Deliberate or not, he was persistent in making you who he needed for his wife, someone compliant. Look at me, Annie."

She moved her eyes from the hearth to his.

"What I want is for you to be you. I have no expectations for you to become anything more than you want to be, but I want you to be the woman who dances to music she enjoys when she's moved to do so. I don't want you to dance or do anything that your heart doesn't long to do. Your life belongs to you now – I'm here, loving you like crazy, hoping you're going to love me too. That's it; I just want you to be fulfilled. You've been fulfilling everyone else for a long time."

Annie didn't smear the tears away. She looked from Shane back to the hearth as if some warmth might spring from that cold, quiet place and save her.

After several moments of silence, Shane's eyes fastened to her face, Annie looked at him and, with both of her hands, smoothed away the moisture from her eyes. "We don't really know one another," she said. "We've touched on our childhoods, your brother's loss, my family's willingness to let me go, but other than that…"

"That's a start, Annie. What more should I tell you? I have absolutely nothing to hide, but neither do I have anything particularly exciting to claim. We'll talk – I love talking to you, I've been hesitant to do that because I thought I'd bore you or that you'd consider my chatter to be invasive. But we've known each other for years, Annie. We might not know details of the past, but you are my present, my future. Nothing else matters to me."

Annie glanced at Sherlock and then back at Shane. "Tell me one thing about you that I don't know."

Shane took a few moments before giving a response. "I hated school."

Annie sat up straighter. "Why? Did something bad happen?"

"No, nothing happened physically or emotionally. That was the problem, I was bored stiff. Some warm days I'd skip school and head to the nearest watering hole for a swim. Other days I would slip into the woods and sit at the base of a huge old pine, watching the comings and goings of birds, squirrels, raccoons, whatever happened by. I did okay with the grades, but nothing outstanding because I was hardly ever there, even when I was there." He smiled as his eyes roamed Annie's lovely face. "What about you? Did you like school?"

"After the first couple of grades I was tutored. There were six of us working with one teacher. Two of the other students with me were Russian. Sometimes the instructor had to go over and over the material so they could understand; it made lessons a little tedious at times."

Shane nodded. "So school wasn't exactly exciting for you either."

"No. I took a few college courses here and there and I liked them, but I had no destination. I was going to dance."

"And dancing, was that fun for you?"

"Sometimes there were days when it was the least of anything I hoped to do. It was expected that I would spend hours in practice and hours in rehearsals. Between dancing and school, I hardly had time to think." Annie hesitated. "It's funny, talking about this makes me realize that my life has been plotted and planned – I wasn't aware of choices."

"What would you have done had you not danced?"

Annie looked away and then back at Shane. "I might have taught first or second grade. I don't know. I remember my first-grade teacher; she was very nice and I liked going to her class. Working at the shelter, with the women and with the children, has shown me that I have something to give. I like that idea."

They sat quietly drinking tepid coffee, each of them reflecting on what had been said. That they had lonely childhoods in common was not difficult to admit. It felt to each of them that they could understand the other – they were children who hadn't been abused, but neither had they been cherished.

Over the next few weeks, Shane calculated that he needed to take things slow with Annie. He had managed to make her comfortable holding his hand as they walked the beach, but not the sidewalks of town.

Annie feared those questioning looks would come from passers-by, from people in shops. She walked with Shane and Sherlock, stopping for coffee and then onto a town bench, Sherlock happily accepting from strangers pats and scratches to his neck and ears.

They became the trio to watch, not because anyone detected an age difference with Annie and Shane, but because they were attractive, sweet-mannered people. Café and shop owners liked them, offered water and treats to Sherlock, and sometimes invited all three inside.

In mid-August, Annie went to her position at the women's shelter.

A couple of hours later Shane heard a car door shut. He went outside and saw Annie limping toward him.

"Hey," Shane said as he and Sherlock greeted her, "what's going on here? What happened to your leg or foot?"

"It's my ankle," Annie said in a frustrated tone. "I was dancing with three children when I stepped on a marble. I tried to correct myself as I began to fall, but instead, I twisted my ankle." She turned back to face the car she'd arrived in. "Thank you so much for the ride, Samantha."

The young woman, seeing that Annie was in good hands, waved, wished Annie well, and drove back to help at the shelter.

"Ice or the doctor?" Shane asked as he reached for her arms and guided her gently to the sofa.

"Oh," she said, "ice in some lemonade, please, and then maybe more ice on this ankle."

"Coming up," he said as he placed an ottoman carefully under her left foot.

For the next few days Annie stayed home as Shane and Sherlock took quick walks through town or to the shore. People asked about Annie and sent wishes for mending well through Shane. Each time someone asked about her, Shane realized how revered she was with her gentle manner and graceful moves.

"That's one lovely woman that wife of yours," a shop owner observed.

Shane smiled and agreed, liking the sound of Annie, his wife.

By the end of August, Annie was walking normally and became visible once again in the community. Everyone had missed her, they asked how she was – it was heartwarming for her to hear the well-wishes. Annie said nothing to Shane, but she recalled a time in New York when she had been similarly injured. No one had noticed her gone, no one inquired about her ankle, and no one said welcome back when she'd healed. There was a difference between living in a small town and blending into a large city. Here she was Annie – there she was just another moving body.

Again on the anniversary of Daisy's death, Annie placed shells and a Marigold plant on the little grave. Shane watched her from the kitchen window where he made coffee, then joined her outside with Sherlock.

"She was special," he said as Annie stood brushing summer soil from her skirt.

Annie turned to pet Sherlock but there was moisture in her eyes. "She saved me," Annie said. "I never thought to have a pet, but she came with the cottage. I didn't know I needed her, but I did. I'm not sure I'd have stayed here without her."

Shane reached out for Annie's hand as they walked back into the house. "I made coffee. Let's have some with fruit and toast and then let's take a ride toward the Cape."

Annie smiled up at him. "Antiquing again?"

"Sure, why not? Sherlock mentioned getting a new collar, something to match the amber of his eyes. I wouldn't mind another something unique in copper, and you haven't had any new earrings for a long while either. Are you game?"

Annie laughed. "Yes, I would absolutely love to go. Are you sure you can take this time from your work?"

"I can. I'm caught up and feeling free."

Seventy miles later, most of it back roads, Annie and Shane had found treasures and were heading home.

Sherlock wore a new collar and had found a chew toy in a pet store which kept him content in the backseat.

"We should use my new flow blue cups and saucers to have coffee tonight," Annie said. "They're so pretty; I can't believe my luck in finding them."

Shane smiled at her. "That's kind of the way I feel about you."

Annie's smile faded and she turned to look at the road ahead.

Shane reached over to the hands folded in her lap. "Hey, how about if we pick up a pizza for dinner?"

She nodded and murmured a soft yes. Shane knew it was time to work on this relationship again in an obvious manner. They needed to share more of their lives – Annie required that connection in order to feel part of another. Everything she had mentioned regarding her husband had been of his doing, his thoughts, his life, all with Annie inserted into it. Shane wanted the life they would make together to be inclusive in every way. What he wanted had to be what Annie wanted – two people looking in the same direction.

"Should we make a salad to go with it?" Annie asked as they pulled up to the pizza shop.

"We could," he said as he turned the ignition switch off. "Or we could be bad and just eat pizza." He smiled and Annie laughed.

"Okay," she said, "lots of pizza."

Sitting at their kitchen table, Sherlock hoping for small pieces of crust, Shane watched as Annie carefully maneuvered the dripping cheese into her beautiful mouth. He loved seeing her consuming something with more calories than her traditional salads – he thought she needed additional flesh on those gorgeous bones.

"Have you been feeling okay?" he asked. "You don't

take those over-the-counter meds any longer, do you?"

Annie wiped the grease from her lips and used her napkin to clean her finger-tips. "I don't take them anymore, strict instructions from my doctor. I feel better, still a little discomfort here and there, but I'm healing."

"Does your doctor agree that you're healing?"

Annie nodded as she reached for her drink. "Yes, the blood work shows less toxicity; I'm making progress."

Shane sat back in his chair and watched her, terrified of losing her.

"Ready for a cup of coffee?" he asked as he stood.

"Yes, out on the porch?"

Shane poured two cups of coffee and placed one before Annie. "Sure," he said. "I'll take Sherlock out for a quick walk, then I'll be back to join you."

Annie stood and lost her balance for just a moment.

Shane noticed and reached for her, steadying her with his hands on her forearms. "You okay?" he asked.

Annie smiled. "I am. Every once-in-a-while I have a little weakness, it doesn't last. It goes with the issue – I'm fine."

Reluctantly he let go of her and watched as she walked to the porch with her coffee. Once she was seated, he attached Sherlock's collar to the leash as they went out. Ten minutes later they were back and Shane sat across from Annie.

With his coffee retrieved from the kitchen he asked, "So, tell me about your first love."

Annie laughed. "Where did that come from? I told you at some time that I had this crush on a young Russian dancer. We were teens. He went back to Russia and I never heard from him again."

"And after that?"

"Nothing exciting. I squeezed in a couple of college

courses while I was dancing, nothing that amounted to anything credit-wise, and I met people my own age, but I didn't really have time to socialize with them. Until Albert, there was nothing much going on in my romantic life."

Shane looked at her and wondered how she'd escaped the arms and hearts of many other dancers and students.

"What about you?" she asked as she placed her cup down.

Shane smiled and said, "Oh, there have been so many, not sure I can remember them all."

Annie smiled in return. "I have no doubt."

Shane took a swallow of coffee then leaned back against the chair's soft cushions. "I had this one girl I liked when I was about sixteen. I kept thinking I should ask her to marry me, then I thought, wait, how do I feed her? I didn't have a dime to my name."

Annie laughed, picturing Shane seriously considering marriage at sixteen. She envisioned him as being a handsome boy with the charm he now possessed. "So, no teen marriage?"

Shane shook his head from side to side. "Nope, I let that one go. Two years later I was in the military – I really haven't had any serious thoughts about anyone, other than you that is."

Annie's eyes met his and her smile faded. "Shane…."

"I know what you're going to say and I'm not listening. More coffee?"

Annie shook her head slowly from side to side, a slight smile of surrender on her lips.

Chapter Fourteen

Annie had never been more content in her life. She felt on the edge of a precipice with her emotional attachment to Shane, but she didn't care. Loving him was excruciatingly delicious and, at the same time, spine-tingling with anticipation of loss. Now when she recalled wishing he'd find a woman his own age with whom to form a loving relationship, she was also reminded that if he did, he'd be gone. She wasn't sure that if that occurred she would be strong enough to endure her vacant heart.

As autumn drifted casually into Salt Hill Bay, days were sprinkled with sunshine and hours of warmth. Nights wore clear skies dotted with trillions of stars and a chill in the air. After daylight walks through town or near the shore, Shane, Annie, and Sherlock were content to settle into their home with lights gleaming, a fire in the hearth. There was, for each of them, a satisfaction in having filled a day with what they chose to do, no more, no less. And at the day's close, a time to relax, reflect, and think a prayerful thank you for the companionship and depth of love.

In her own bed each night, Sherlock at her side, she scanned the light from her window. Full moons were her favorite, as if Mother Nature had hung her lantern and was about to make her rounds. Nights when only the stars were visible, or none of them due to hovering clouds, Annie looked into the darkness until her thoughts faded and her eyes closed. She thought of Shane; he was a sort of miracle in her life, an introduction to genuine love and a new reality for who she was. Annie wondered if this was the cumulative affection teenaged girls felt for their first love, a kind of light-filled giddiness for another being. She smiled as she thought of herself as a late-bloomer, feeling and falling in love at the age of forty-nine, and carrying that love with her into sixty.

An observant child, Annie had been aware of her mother's graying hair and her grandmother's of snow white. She had always thought that as one grew older, thoughts of romance surely lessened. Now she knew better and, if anything, that intensity grew.

Shane very often did not immediately drift off to sleep. Pain sometimes had a way of infiltrating his plans for rest, and then there was Annie. In the shadowy room with slivers of light seeping in to paint the walls a lighter shade, he thought about the room itself, bereft of Annie's personal touches other than attractive bedding and simple white curtains. He thought about the other rooms in this sweet cottage by the sea, rooms which reflected a feminine glow, nothing to indicate a man's choice. Had Annie secured this existence, eliminating the presence of her husband intentionally? Always, she had spoken of Albert respectfully, a take-charge individual who had influenced her life to the point of stardom in the dancing world. Surely Annie was grateful, but had there been a complete fulfillment in this marriage of mind and talent? There had been no plans for children; Albert had determined that in their cosmopolitan life, there was no room for the distraction of little ones. Apparently, Annie had not resisted.

With his arms bent, his hands propped between the

pillow and the back of his head, Shane looked to the darkened windows and realized that although he should be tired, he wasn't. He moved the covers away and sat on his bed's edge, slipped his feet into slippers, then stood and reached for the one small light. What now? he wondered.

In his closet on a shelf there were two ample cardboard boxes. Annie had told him they were just old things and to leave them there unless he needed more space. Now Shane wondered about those old things, if they were hers or possibly Albert's.

At the closet, he was careful about not making noise and waking Annie on the other side of the wall. He reached for one carton, placing it on his bed, then the other, settling it next to the first. He hesitated: was this an intrusion of her privacy? Yes, he determined it was.

He walked to the window and looked out at the dark, vague figures of pines and distant street lights. He turned and looked at the two cartons, considering their fate. He sat down next to them on his bed and stared at the folded over tops. Clothing? Sheet music? Shane ran his left hand through thick hair then rubbed his chin as he closed his eyes. When he opened his eyes again and sat up straight, he reached for the top of the box closest to him. One flap after the other was lifted until all four were open, exposing a length of tissue. He lifted the tissue and stared at a variety of papers; some were sheet music as he suspected, some were letters tied with narrow black ribbon postmarked from Austria. Shane moved his hand to touch the letter on top then withdrew his hand as if he'd approached fire.

He sat back and took a deep breath, wondering if this was a grave-robbing expedition. After moments, he reached for the first letter, opening the envelope carefully. Folded in half, the letter was written in brown ink with precision hand-writing. It began:

Dearest Albert,

The money order arrived this morning exactly on the date you have always determined. It is a blessing, knowing that we can appropriately care for what is important to us all.

The rains have come, leaving this old house feeling chilled. We light the gas fires nightly and find solace in sitting by the light to read. The village is quiet, only those who need to go out into this weather are there. No strollers pass, no friendly waves.

Prayers for you as you continue with your talent-filled life in that grand city of New York.

With thanks and affection,

Mama

Shane read the letter then read it again. He wondered as he glanced around the room what she referred to as "important to us all." He recalled Annie saying that Albert sent money back home regularly, but what was his mother's meaning of important? Shane folded the letter and reached for another two or three letters down.

My Dearest Son,

Your generous money order arrived today and it was a wonderful relief. The nurse has asked for an increase in her salary and, while she does deserve it, it is a concern I think of daily, keeping your son comfortable and in good health. In his twenty-third year, he still does not speak, yet he tries.

Shane dropped the letter to his lap and formed the word 'what?' on his lips. Albert had a son? Did Annie know about this? If she did, why had she not mentioned it?

We do not hear from Lisbetta. It is like the two of you

were unknown to one another, never had a child. I find it sad that she does not choose to visit her son. That he was born imperfect should not affect a mother's love.

Thank you again, my dear Albert. I think of you daily as I look into the eyes of the boy who shares your likeness.

Loving prayers for you,
Mama

Shane held the thin page and read it again. *Lisbetta. Who was Lisbetta? Had she been Albert's wife?* Shane left the letter on his bed and walked around the room. He returned to the letter, folded it away and left the box as he'd found it.

He stood and looked at the two cartons. What secrets could they hold? How much did Annie know about this?

He placed each brown box back on the shelf over his hanging clothes and quietly shut the closet door. Pulling slippers from his feet, he reached to shut off the light and moved his legs beneath the covers, sliding down into the bed where he stared at the shadowed ceiling. Why, he wondered, would Annie not have mentioned this, that Albert had a son, and then this Lisbetta, seemingly the son's mother? Did Annie know?

Part of Shane's heart ached for the possibility of deceit from Albert to Annie. The one photo Shane saw of Albert revealed a confident, handsome man with the look of determination in his eyes. Had he been grooming Annie all those years to be the accepting woman in his life? *She will dance as I direct, she will stand at my side as I mold her into the woman I need her to be.* Or was Shane imagining the arrogance of Annie's former husband? It was possible, he thought, that Albert had shared these letters and the son's existence with Annie, that she knew everything. But, did she?

139

Shane turned from his back to his side and closed his eyes. Annie had managed to build a life with Albert, but did she truly know the man who had been her husband? While Shane knew that would never be a deliberate route for her to take, it was still troubling. What if she didn't know? What if she had respected Albert's privacy by never touching these boxes? But then why would she have saved them when everything else of Albert seemed to be gone? Not a shirt, not a tie, not a single personal item belonging to Albert existed in that small house. Yet here sat these bundles of years fastened together with black satin ribbon encased in a burial box.

A burial box, a pair of them. Shane questioned his thoughts. He could not help but wonder if he wanted to believe that Annie was through mourning her husband's loss. Truth be known, Shane had no desire to share her with man or ghost. He reviewed the little cottage she had selected for her life – the carefully selected books on the shelves, the pale colored walls, the fireplace mantle and tables dotted with seashells and small, colorful rocks. This place was Annie and, from what she had told him, the large brownstone in New York had been formal, filled with lavish furniture and decorative art forms chosen by Albert before Annie. This cottage, he thought, is almost like a denial that there had ever been anything or anyone else to influence how she chose to live. This was her statement.

As thoughts formed in questions faded away, sleep came for Shane and the morning brought it all back like a pounding thunder. He sat up in bed, swung his legs to the floor, and rubbed his face lightly. He stood, casting the covers aside, then turned and pulled them into place the way Annie liked to keep her house, neat, uncluttered.

Later in the kitchen, he poured himself a cup of hot

140

coffee and glanced into the living room where Annie sat with Sherlock at her side.

"Good morning," she said with a smile and slight wave of her left hand. "You must have been having sweet dreams to keep you in bed later than usual."

Shane nodded and made his way into the room, sitting down across from her. Sherlock looked at Annie, as if to ask permission, then slowly moved to greet Shane with a nudge from his large head. Shane stroked the dog's neck and ears, then sat back and sipped the hot brew as his eyes met Annie's.

"Have you been up long?"

Annie smiled. "A few hours."

"Hours?" Shane questioned. "What time is it?"

Annie laughed. "It's after ten."

"Whoa, I guess I am late getting up. About three hours late."

Annie smiled and sipped her coffee. "You must have needed the sleep."

Shane gave no explanation for his late arrival into morning. "Did you go for a walk?" he asked.

Annie held her cup with both hands and looked at him. His hair was tousled from bed and his attire consisted of bare feet, jeans, and a black t-shirt. "I was waiting for you, but Sherlock and I would be happy to join you if you're interested in a walk at the beach."

Shane knew he should get to work, there was an expected project online, but he would take that walk with Annie. Maybe it would clear his mind.

"I'll go," he said. "Let me gulp down the rest of my coffee and I'll grab some shoes."

On the moist sand, the three walked, Sherlock occasionally dashing toward a seagull or chasing a wave. Annie pulled her hip-length jacket closer to her chest and fastened the last button toward her throat. Wind caught her shoulder-length hair and tossed it about, causing her to frequently push it aside. Shane looked at her and smiled. She was the epitome of perfection, not just in appearance, but in her demeanor.

"Cold?" he asked.

Annie shook her head. "Not really, it's just that time of year, autumn bluster here and there. It feels invigorating actually. I love the seasons, snow and all.

"Are you good with soup?" she questioned out of the blue.

Shane nodded. "I love soup. What do you have in mind?"

Annie shrugged her lean shoulders. "Not sure, just thought it was feeling like soup weather. I know how to make turkey gumbo, and I do a pretty good corn chowder. Any preference?"

Shane looked down at her diminutive form and wanted to gather her up in his arms. Instead, he moved along the shoreline keeping his steps in time with hers. "The gumbo sounds good, but either would be great. You know I love your corn chowder. Make me some soup, woman!"

Annie looked up at him and laughed. "Really? That's the manners I should expect from you?"

Shane reached out one arm and gathered her to him. "Sorry, couldn't resist. Shall we turn about and head home?"

Annie nodded and did nothing to remove herself from his firm grasp. He was warm to lean against, and the penetration of that warmth seemed to vibrate through her body like a racecar zooming around a track.

Shane whistled for Sherlock who was nosing his way along the shallow water. The dog turned and galloped toward them as they headed back toward town and home. They were a family; untraditional in stance, and yet theirs was solid and cohesive as any relationship could be.

Shane felt compelled to ask Annie about her marriage to Albert. The knowledge of him having a child back in Austria was daunting, and now he wondered how Annie would react if she knew, or had she known all along?

Washing and drying dishes together after making and consuming turkey gumbo, Shane asked, "So, you and Albert decided together that there would be no children?"

Annie seemed taken aback by the question. "Well, yes. It was reasonable for our lifestyle in New York."

"And," Shane continued carefully, "Albert had never been married before, he had no children before he met you?"

Annie's eyes were on the suds from washing a large tureen when she smiled at Shane slightly. "None that he ever told me about."

Shane struggled not to drop one of their soup bowls. He dried it and placed it back into a cupboard and then he was quiet. *She didn't know.*

Chapter Fifteen

Shane had many thoughts concerning how secretive Albert had been with Annie. He felt angry at times for the possible deceit, and then he would reason why a man would not simply reveal a former wife or girlfriend, or a child. Nothing made sense. He began to feel that Albert might have been a self-serving individual who took what he wanted from life and left behind what could be construed as unwanted baggage. Shane wasn't sure he would have liked Annie's Albert.

Closer to the holidays, Annie mentioned Thanksgiving, plans for preparing a meal together and walking through town. She talked about Christmas, too, the little tree they'd enjoyed years ago that had then been planted at the back edge of her garden. She wanted another tree, another warm and wonderful Christmas with Shane and Sherlock at her side.

"I've been thinking," she began one afternoon as they chopped vegetables for a pizza.

"Oh, oh," he said with a smile, "what kind of trouble are you dreaming up now?"

Annie flipped a slice of yellow pepper at him and put one hand on her hip.

"Okay, you have my attention," he said. "What's going on in that gorgeous head of yours?"

"Christmas," she said.

Shane laughed. "We haven't even had Thanksgiving."

"I know," she said, "but Christmas takes planning, more plans than Thanksgiving. I guess I'm wondering, are you going to stay here for Christmas?"

Shane stopped slicing a sweet onion and looked at her. "There is no place in the world I'd rather be other than here, Annie. Do you have a plan?" he asked as he resumed slicing.

Annie moved to the sink to wash her hands. As she dried them she looked at Shane's profile as he continued to slice the onion. "Nothing huge, just wondered about getting a tree the way we did once before."

Shane stopped what he was doing and looked at her. "You didn't get a tree those years we were apart?"

Annie hesitated then said no.

Shane looked at her with sadness reflected in his eyes. He said nothing until several moments passed. "We are definitely having a tree. I was thinking a good fake – something we could put up at Thanksgiving without worrying about keeping it watered and fresh. We could enjoy it longer, what do you think?"

Annie swallowed back tears. It was enough to know that Shane would be there with her and that large dog, celebrating the joy of life. "An artificial tree would be fine," she said, "as long as we have natural greens around the house. Balsam smells so good."

"Sounds like a plan," he said as he scraped the onion slices onto a pizza dough ready for the oven. He glanced at Annie who wore the sweetest smile, like a child who had just been told they were going to play at the park. He wanted to take her in his arms and hold her tight, but this would need the right time and place. He took a deep breath after placing the pizza into the oven, stunned with the realization and depth of his love for this woman.

"Annie," he said, so softly that she was not sure he spoke, "I can't wait for Christmas. The one I shared with you and Daisy was the best. Now we have this gigantic dog, and I'm not going anywhere, not now, not ever."

Annie's hands covered her face and he moved toward her, taking her hands down and wrapping them around his neck. He looked into her tear-filled eyes and then drew her close. "I'm here to stay, Annie," he whispered into her hair at the base of her neck.

Thanksgiving brought sunshine, cold, and a parade through town. Shane and Annie had prepared food and left it in the oven to cook while they took Sherlock out to the festivities. Invigorated with their walk and the bright colored theme of the day, they returned to the house which met them with aroma and an awakened appetite.

"Oh," Shane began as he took Annie's coat and hung it with his, "do you think it gets any better than this? It smells so good in here."

Annie smiled and rubbed her hands as she walked toward the kitchen to check the oven.

"What would you say to a fire in the hearth while we dine?" he asked. "We could eat in the living room; I can move the small table from my room front and center."

Annie nodded. "Yes, that would be lovely; let's do it."

The next day, a six-foot artificial tree was purchased, tiny white lights were strung, and ornaments were carefully placed – they would have weeks to enjoy the soft, celebratory lights of Christmas.

Shane watched Annie's actions, always wondering what she was thinking. How did she spend those many Christmases in New York? He decided they were probably elegant occasions with lavish foods and expensive gifts, acquaintances dropping by for a glass of fine wine or an aged whiskey. None of that seemed to go with Annie's demeanor. This little cottage with its modesty and simple fare suited her. He thought again of Albert; how could that man not have told his beautiful young wife about a child he left behind in Austria?

Shane resolved that this Christmas was going to be the best – life was unpredictable and each moment would matter. He thought about a gift for Annie and decided he knew what he would search for. She was his love; what brightened her heart would bring an intense brilliance to their lives; there was nothing more important to him than making her happy.

Annie collected her memories of times when Shane touched her to tease or console. Every one of those times felt new, exciting, necessary. Fighting the emotions too long, she at last could concede to herself that she was romantically in love with this man, seventeen years younger no longer first on her mind. Now she wondered how to proceed; it was not her style to tell him in words. She would find ways to reveal her love.

"Tell me," Shane said as they dined on Thanksgiving leftovers with Sherlock at their side, "how you spent Christmases as a child."

Annie drew a napkin to her lips as she slipped a small morsel of food to the patient dog. "On the farm? It was honestly like most days. My father and I collected fresh eggs from the chickens and my mother made breakfast. Everything had to be done, all the chores, before we were allowed sweet tea and gifts from the tree."

"Sweet tea?"

Annie smiled. "Mother thought that if children drank tea, it should be laced with milk and honey to add nutrition. It was a treat."

Shane sat back in his chair and looked at the face of

the woman he loved, the only woman he had *ever* loved. "And then the gifts were opened?"

Annie cocked her head to one side then looked at Shane. "Yes, the gifts. Little things, not like what kids today expect. It was very reasonable that an old man in red could arrive in a sleigh, climb down a chimney, and leave what we received: a small doll or pretty ribbons to tie in our hair. Handmade mittens were always there, socks, a new dress, a bit of our favorite candies from a store." Annie smiled at Shane. "It was magical, every single bit of it."

"And in New York?"

Annie's smile disappeared. "It was different. I couldn't go home for the holidays because that's when the most extravagant performances took place as a dancer. I would receive a small parcel from home, and a few people involved with the ballet company gave us items like new ballet slippers, new dancing leotards. It was just different."

Shane watched her face go from a soft glee in talking about Christmas on the farm to a city experience with acquaintances.

"And with your husband, it must have been a gala with your positions in life."

Annie looked down and then up into Shane's grey eyes. "Albert had the house decorated by a professional. It was beautiful. The tree was fifteen feet high, the centerpiece of the entrance to the house. Sometimes I felt like I was on stage as I entered; it was all so perfect."

Perfect. That's what she'd said, but what did that mean? Shane considered that she meant to describe everything in order, a managed event. This woman he loved would not be impressed by glamor and bright lights.

"How did you spend Christmas Eve and day?"

Annie took a deep breath. "Friends came on Christmas Eve for drinks. I usually slipped away to call home. Christmas Day Albert insisted on early morning church and then home. We would give one another one gift – he thought that was appropriate and I was fine with that. I wanted for nothing. It was another day." She shrugged her shoulders and reached for her coffee cup. "What about you? What kind of Christmases did you have?"

Shane reached down to pat Sherlock. "I had a farm life, too. Chores had to be done before even a sip of water. My mother orchestrated the meal and the gifts; Dad was sort of removed. She bought us new boots, sometimes a sled if one was needed; we had a few toys, but mostly practical clothing items. I remember it as being warm, nice cinnamon rolls for breakfast with eggs. Mom tried. It was good."

"How about in New Mexico? What did you do on Christmas?"

Shane looked out through a window and then back at Annie. "Not much. My friends all had family to go to; I was usually on my own; another day, another dollar."

Annie sat back in her chair holding her coffee cup in both hands. She understood the lonely effect the holidays could cast on a day when you seemed to be out of step with expectations. She and Shane had similar childhoods, and even adulthoods. Now things could be different; they were capable of generating a Christmas filled with what they wanted: being together.

"Hey," Shane interrupted her thoughts, "we'll have to get this kid here a good present." He looked down at Sherlock and gave the dog's ears a gentle pull.

Annie smiled. "Oh yes, Sherlock loves a new toy, and

last year I bought him his pretty blue collar and matching leash as well. He also had four broiled scallops for part of his dinner. We shared."

Shane smiled and looked into Annie's pale blue eyes. "We're going to have an amazing Christmas."

Annie felt a rush of warmth flow through her body. She had faith in Shane's words and belief in what she felt. The years between them began to feel insignificant. Now was all that mattered.

Annie stood and moved her chair toward the table, reaching for her plate and then Shane's. "We can let the dishes soak while we have another coffee by this glorious fire, and maybe later, a slice of pie."

Shane stood and gathered more dishes to take to the kitchen. "How about a little warm brandy instead of the coffee?"

Annie smiled. "Yes, that sounds good."

Within moments, the table set before the hearth was cleared and brandy was warmed and poured. They sat opposite one another, neither of them wanting to rush what they felt. Shane knew that at some point soon, he was going to take this woman in his arms. Annie knew that he would and that resistance would be nonexistent. It was awkward, but they were ready.

"Pie?" Annie asked later as the brandy had disappeared and the fire was low.

"Sure, but let me take Sherlock out again for a watering. You cut the pie – I'll be right back."

Sleepily, Annie slipped out of her chair and walked to the kitchen as Shane pulled a jacket on and snapped Sherlock's leash into place. Ten minutes later he walked back into the house, shed the jacket, and unclipped Sherlock setting him free. Immediately, the dog walked to the kitchen with intent in his stride.

The table was empty; Shane called to Annie. She answered softly as he walked to the kitchen where he found her left hand in a red-stained clump of paper towels.

"My God, Annie! What happened?" He moved swiftly to her side and took her hand, its blood dripping onto his fingers.

"I broke one of the brandy snifters," she said softly. "It's not deep."

With his left hand beneath hers, he wrapped his right arm around her waist and directed her to a kitchen chair. "Sit down," he said gently. "Let's take a better look at this."

Seated, with her hand on the table, a dish towel and paper towels underneath the wound, Shane rushed to the medicine cabinet for iodine, an antibiotic ointment, and some bandages. He held clean paper towels in place to help stop the bleeding and questioned whether they should go to the hospital for stitches. Annie declined saying that she would be okay, the bleeding would stop in time.

Shane pulled a chair close to her and sat down, holding her slim wrist as he watched the blood further stain the white material. When the blood flow ceased, he examined the one-inch wound and dabbed it with iodine. Without causing further blood to escape, he applied a layer of ointment and then wrapped her hand in bandages.

Annie watched him and felt the gentleness of his touch. His concern and care was tender; she was tempted to reach out to him, to draw him close. Tears spilled from her eyes and she tried to whisk them away before he could see.

He noticed the movement and then the tell-tale stains

on her beautiful face. Without a word, he leaned forward and hugged her.

"Does it hurt?" he asked.

Annie shook her head from side to side.

"You're traumatized," he said. "You're coming with me. Come on, I'm taking you into the living room where you can sit comfortably while I make you some tea."

Without a further word from either of them, Annie was moved slowly to the sofa where she sat, a small pillow elevating her hand.

"Shane," she called to him as he was leaving the room, "could we have tea in my flow blue cups? I was going to use them with our evening coffee."

Shane smiled. "You trust me to handle your beautiful cups and saucers?"

"Yes, I do."

After tea by a blazing hearth, Sherlock was walked one last time for the evening. Shane stepped into the house and noted Annie's sleepy look as he unsnapped the leash from the large dog and went to Annie. She opened her eyes and smiled up at him.

"Come on, little girl, I think you need your bed. We've had a long, great day. It's time to rest."

"It's only nine o'clock," she protested.

"Sounds like bedtime to me," he said.

Annie hesitated and looked away.

"What, Annie? What's wrong?"

At first she was silent and then she spoke softly. "Does everyone think I'm incapable of making decisions? It seems so."

Shane stood up straight, taking his hand away from where he'd placed it on her arm. He took a deep breath. Yes, her life had been a continuing arrangement by others and she was tired of it.

"Annie," he said softly as he squatted down before her, "I'm not telling you what to do. Please accept my apology if it seemed that way. I get it; people have been engineering your life all along. I'm not here to do that. I'm here because we met for a purpose. I love you, Annie, and all I want right now is for you to be okay. I'm sorry."

Annie brushed a stray tear from her cheek and sat up straight on the sofa. "No," she said, "I'm the one who should be sorry. You've been wonderful, Shane. I think you're right; I'm tired and this cut into my hand did add unneeded trauma to an otherwise perfect day. I'll get ready for bed."

Shane stood and reached out to help her up then walked with her into her room. She started to unbutton her blouse and found it awkward, until Shane offered to help. With slow movement of his lean fingers, careful not to brush her pale skin, he unfastened the buttons on her blouse and then the button to her long skirt, unzipping the side while watching her eyes.

Annie trembled and he could feel that imperceptible action beneath his fingers.

Before he could go any further Annie told him there was a nightdress in the top drawer of her dresser. He found a knee-length garment in pale gray jersey and held it for her to see. She nodded and he took it to her, slipping it over her head so that she could discreetly remove her other clothing; he did not offer help. As she stepped out of her skirt, Annie lost her balance and stumbled against the footboard of the bed. Shane reached out and steadied her. For moments, they were in one another's arms, silent. "I'm okay," she said softly.

"I'm staying," he said, with neither of them thinking that this was one of those times when someone took over her life against her wishes.

From the moment when Annie was settled into her nightwear, Shane took her gently by the shoulders and urged her to bed. Once she was in and covered, Shane disappeared into his own room, returning wearing lounge pajama bottoms and a short sleeved t-shirt. Annie had her eyes closed as she lay in a fetal position on her right side, until she felt the weight on her bed. She opened her eyes and turned to see Shane pulling up covers over himself as he molded his lean body next to hers.

"Shane," she began in protest.

"I can't hear you," he said. "Sleep, Annie. I'm not here for any other reason except to hold that hand of yours so that you won't move it around too much; I'm afraid it could start bleeding again."

Annie relaxed her breathing, closed her eyes, and felt the warmth from his body against hers. Nothing had ever felt more intimate. In moments she was asleep, his left hand around hers, keeping it reliably stable.

He could barely hear her breathing yet felt the slight rise and fall of her breath as his left arm rested softly across her hips. With his face lightly pressed against her hair, he closed his eyes and dared to move so that every part of his body was touching hers. For years, yes, he thought, there had been other women, but no one he'd loved. Annie deserved to be loved in the manner he felt capable of expressing.

They slept, seemingly dreamless, with gentle movements adjusting them compatibly. When Annie woke in the morning, Shane was gone and the aroma of coffee wafted into her room. She smiled with the memory of him beside her all night and the anticipation for what the new day would bring.

Chapter Sixteen

The Saturday night after Thanksgiving, they sat in the darkened living room with the glow from the hearth and the tree illuminating their faces. Shane had made salad and pizza, good-naturedly forbidding Annie to do more than watch as he sliced and diced vegetables. With dinner served in the living room, coffee in Annie's blue and white cups completed the meal. For Annie, the day could not have been more joyful.

"Look at us," Shane said, sitting at one end of Annie's sofa, "you, me, and this massive dog. Aren't we something?"

Annie laughed. "I suppose we are."

Shane stood and moved closer to Annie so that he could hold her right hand. "Suppose nothing," he said. "We're awesome, all three of us."

Annie laughed again and did nothing about withdrawing her hand from his.

"Should we walk?" she asked.

"I think we should stay right here where it's warm and cozy. I'll take Sherlock out again in a bit, but," he shook his head, "it's pretty nice right here."

Annie smiled as she agreed. "The tree is beautiful, you decorated it well; everything is evenly placed."

When Shane gently squeezed her hand, it sent electric shocks through Annie's body. *Where is this coming from?* How, she wondered, could a woman her age not know about these endearing emotions until now? She began to think about age again and then stopped. If he didn't care about the seventeen years of life she'd known before he was born, she wouldn't either. She understood that for her, in many ways, life began when she met this magical man on the beach.

"What would you like to plan for Christmas?" he asked, looking at her luminous eyes.

Annie thought for a few moments. This had not been a decision she'd thought about in many years, not since last being with Shane. "Do you mean for us, the three of us?"

Shane laughed. "Yes, the three of us; other than a walk, weather permitting, a nice dinner, and a few surprises under the tree, what would you like to do?"

Annie was pensive. "I don't know. Maybe we could take some mittens, scarves, and gloves over to the women's center. This time of year is hard for them. Some find their way home, if even for just the day, but others have no place to go. We could take them little gifts."

"You haven't been there in a while, do you think it would be a good idea to call and see how many are there?"

Annie sighed. "Yes, I'll do that. I feel so guilty for not feeling up to the dance instruction. When I began to have this stomach issue, I lost more than good health."

"And now?" he asked. "Are you feeling better? I don't think you've put on an ounce since I came back."

Annie grimaced and then smiled. "I'm getting there, and I don't take those over-the-counter pills anymore; all is well."

Shane raised his eyebrows as he looked toward the tree. "I hope so. Does your doctor think you're doing better?"

Annie nodded. "Yes, the discomfort has definitely diminished. I'm much better. It's all your good cooking, I'm sure."

When Sherlock moved to the floor, Shane wrapped his arm around her shoulders, gathering her closer to him. "You took care of me for months after my surgeries. It's my turn to watch over you, and I love every minute." He lightly kissed her forehead, squeezed her hand again, then offered a hot drink. With her acceptance, he brought her tea in one of her blue and white cups.

"We'll need a day out shopping," Shane began as he sat down next to Annie. "Would you like to head north this time? We could go to Boston, New Hampshire, or keep it local. What do you think?"

Annie took a swallow of the hot tea then balanced the cup and saucer on her lap. "I would love to go north," she said, "just for the ride into the mountains, but for shopping, we could keep it local."

Shane nodded. "Sounds good; let's do both. We can have a day or two up north with Sherlock as our chaperone, and another day here in town for a little shopping."

Annie took another sip of tea and looked at the tiny lights on their tree. She had never done anything like this before. As a child in Connecticut, if shopping was done at all, it did not include an excursion for children. In New York, she selected small items of gloves and jewelry to send home, and later with Albert it was all his suggestions for each of them. No surprises among their gifts.

"You know what? I'm going to take this mutt out for a brief walk and then we can curl up for the evening, right here with TV or a book, or early to bed. Think about it –

I'll be back in about ten minutes," he said as he stood.

Annie watched him slip into a jacket then clip Sherlock's leash in place. She smiled at the thought that these two were her own. As the door closed, allowing a rush of cold wind into the room, Annie shivered then thought about Albert. *I will always be guilty of not loving him. He was certain I would in time, and while I grew to care, I did not learn to love and thought I never would. I was wrong. I loved, but not Albert. I love the one who waited.* It was Shane who awakened her heart.

Annie finished her tea then took the cup and saucer to the kitchen. She stood at her window looking out to the darkened garden and thought about all the love that lingered there; little Daisy beneath a shallow grave adorned with shells and winsome stones from the sea. Crisp stems whose blooms had perished with the cold, the small bird feeders. All had vanished in the dark, yet they were solidly there. She thought again of Albert, his grave in New York, visited by his admirers, but by no one who actually loved him. She tried, but it had begun to feel as if her life had been a scheme. Deceit was heavy; Annie found herself resenting her introduction to the world of ballet fame. How important was that to a person's self-acceptance?

As Annie dried her cup and saucer, Shane walked into the kitchen with Sherlock at his heels. He looked at Annie and smiled as she turned to face him. About to ask how their walk was, she instead questioned, "What?"

Shane laughed. "I just get a kick out of you. Standing there with your hair pulled into a ponytail, you look so young and vulnerable. Like, about thirteen."

Annie smiled and scowled at the same time. "Thirteen? Seventeen would have seemed so much more, you know, appealing."

Shane took two steps toward her and pulled her into his arms for a hug. "Annie, do I detect a wishful thought for being alluring?"

She did not reply as she felt herself warmly embraced and enjoying it.

"Annie," he whispered into her hair, "you're alluring. You're more than that, you're enchanting."

She moved just enough to loosen the grasp they had on one another. "We need to be discreet in front of Sherlock," she said. "He's very perceptive you know."

Shane understood that Annie was feeling ill at ease with her closeness to him. He would work on that – perhaps with a more subtle maneuver than simply reaching out and grabbing her. He smiled as he slipped his hands from her waist to her upper arms and then moved a step back. He wanted to comment, to say *some day soon,* but he said nothing.

Annie felt warmth creep onto her face and turned away to fuss with placing dishes back in the cupboard. Try as she might to prevent seeming gracefully fragile as the ballet dancer, Annie moved deliberately faster than usual. She wanted to fit in, to not be Annasheeva as much as simply Annie.

"Are you interested in TV," Shane asked. "Or are you up to reading or playing a game?"

Annie turned toward him with a smile. "A game?"

"Yeah. I saw Scrabble sitting on a lower shelf under some books in the living room."

Annie nodded. "A dancer friend of mine, Eloise, gave that to me. We played a few times during quiet evenings after a performance. I haven't played in years."

"Is that fear I hear?"

Annie gave Shane a quick glance. "Fear? Of what?"

Shane rested his hands on his hips. "Fear of losing."

"To whom?" she replied with a smirk on her otherwise serene face.

"That does it," he said as he moved to the living room where he placed the game on the trunk before the sofa. "Come on," he said, "I'll show you how this is done."

Annie laughed as she sat down next to him. "I wouldn't be so smug if I were you, but I'll allow you this warning. Anyone who played this game with me knew I liked the aesthetics more than winning."

Shane looked at her as he set up the game, handing her the small bag containing wooden letters. "And exactly what does that mean?"

"I like the board to be balanced, all four corners being used."

"So you play to lose," he teased.

Annie laughed. "I love to win, but being focused on how the board looks, I seldom do."

"Sounds like a deal for me," he said. "Choose your letters, woman. You're about to get skunked."

Annie put her head back for a moment in laughter. "Skunked, huh? That's a new term for me to digest."

He gave her a look laden with warning.

"Maybe I'll surprise you," she said as she reached into the small velvet bag for seven tiles.

Annie won that game, laughing at her good fortune in selecting high-value letters. Shane smiled and promised that next time he'd be tough on her.

In her bed, the covers pulled up to her chest, Annie smiled. Shane was fun – she wondered how she'd managed without him for so long. No one, except perhaps her family when she was very young, made her feel the value of being herself until Shane. It had always been about her lithe form, her agility and grace, the in sync movements of her body married to the music.

Chapter Seventeen

Shane stretched out in bed thinking he was tired and sleep would come easily. After minutes of staring at the ceiling, his hands behind his head, he realized that his mind had other plans. He thought about Annie, how much he yearned to hold her close, to love her in a way he felt certain she had not known. She was innocent, old world in a sense. He understood that he could be wrong, but he believed that Albert had been with Annie as he ruled her life, with his best intentions, but still self-serving. Shane could envision taking this woman he loved into a realm of passion.

He turned onto his left side, facing a window, then turned to his right side, facing the closet and those intriguing boxes filled with what was left of Albert. It annoyed Shane that that man had a life he'd left behind in another land, a son. Why would he do such a thing?

Shane sat up and then stood. He was motionless as he stared at the blank closet door, sure that he should not invade the ghostly life tucked away in those boxes.

Quietly, carefully, he opened the door and reached for one carton, setting it on his bed. He sat down next to it and stared at the closed top. It was several minutes before he felt his fingers tugging at the cardboard corners, lifting the tissue paper on top, revealing the letters. He untied the black ribbon and moved the first two letters he had read. He skipped the next few envelopes until he came to one that had an especially decorative stamp. The return address was the same as the others, the apparent street and home of Albert's mother. He unfolded a letter and held it without looking at its cursive writing. After a deep breath, he began to read.

My Dearest Son,

Your letter and funds arrived this morning. I thank you, as always.

Your boy is enjoying the benefit of your thought as he quietly watches old films and sips tea. He is content with simple pleasures.

I have thought so often of you over the years, wishing to see your face. I understand that your life in America is what you need, and to know that you are well is satisfying to some degree.

When you write of your beloved dancer, I can almost see her moving to your music, bringing all your hopes and dreams to fruition. She must be lovely. How kind of her to accommodate your talents, to bring your work to life. Perhaps some day you'll bring her here. Austria is a beautiful country that she would be certain to enjoy. Of course, I would love to see you, my son; that is my greatest hope.

With my heartfelt longing for you and best of wishes,
Mama

How sad, Shane thought as he held the letter in his hands. This woman longed to see her son, and for reasons known to Albert alone, he stayed away from Austria and a child he left in his mother's care. How could he have managed kindness to Annie when he was not considerate of his own mother?

Shane's thoughts and questions always drew him to Annie, her elegant form and face equal to her demeanor.

What, he wondered, persuaded Albert to keep this remarkable woman from his family? The child he kept hidden in his homeland? It did not seem viable that he could have concealed a former life from Annie, his protégé, his wife.

Shane slipped another envelope from the collection and unfolded a letter revealing an unfamiliar writing style. This was one from Albert to his mother. How, Shane pondered, did a letter from Albert end up among letters from his mother? Shane sifted through the remaining letters to see if there were more from Annie's former husband. There were not. Then he looked through the second box; again, finding nothing other than letters from Albert's mother. Slowly, with trepidation, Shane began to read the letter from Albert, dated just three years after his marriage to Annie.

Dear Mama,

The enclosed includes an extra amount to compensate for the approaching holidays. Please purchase something fine for my son and yourself.

You have been curious about my infatuation with Annasheeva. She is a woman you would be enriched to know. Her skills on stage are breathtaking; her interpretation of my music is like no other. I dare not blink for fear of missing even one moment of her dancing. She, among other performers, has been the moon to the stars – she understands the importance of every note's inclusion. She, as no other could, has made my life.

Shane glimpsed over the remaining paragraph pertaining to Albert's thanks for all his mother had undertaken in the care of his son. Shane read the letter again then folded it back into its envelope. He sat on the edge of his bed, drawing his hands over his thighs in angered emotion. This man, Albert, had used Annie to perfectly translate his music – it was all about his needs, not Annie's.

In two quick motions the cartons were placed back on the closet shelf, like returning the body to the grave. Shane walked the perimeter of his room, stopping at the window facing the street. *How could Annie not know? Where did this letter come from? It had obviously been mailed to Austria; how did it end up in with the mail from his mother?*

Shane paced around the room, confused and feeling protective. Annie was delicate in form; wasn't she also fragile in thought?

Sleep did not come easy. Shane's mind tossed and mingled thoughts of Annie's life. How, he wondered, had so many people forfeited the girl, the woman, to extract from her the obvious, natural talent? As a child, surely she was treasured. How does a parent, a family let a child go to live far away for the sake of a career? How does a grown, successful man find it acceptable to physically and mentally cage a being for his own reward?

Annie woke from a sound sleep and noted that it was after four in the morning. She listened for any sounds but could hear only the breathing of the large dog settled by her feet. She smiled at the long form and sweet face then turned on her side. She thought about Shane and knew: without him, life would not be nearly so reassuring. She thought about sharing coffee with him in just two or three hours, smiled, then closed her eyes, pulled the covers closer to her chin, and returned to sleep.

With morning light, they found one another in the brief hallway, Annie wrapped in a pale blue satin garment, the belt tied at her slender waist. Shane looked at her tousled hair and wanted to pull that woman into his arms and take her right back to the bedroom, his or hers, it didn't matter.

Annie smiled at him, genuinely glad to be starting the day with him over coffee and their light conversations. The fluttering inside the core of her body felt familiar, a typical reaction to being close to Shane, to love. Had she not known this before? She tried to think of who might have brought forth these feelings and could not. Except for people and pets she'd accumulated as a child, and her beloved Daisy, Annie could think of no other love from her past.

"French toast this morning?" he asked.

Annie raised her eyebrows and smiled at him. "Sounds extravagant, let's; I'll make the coffee."

Shane thought about reaching out to tug her hair in a tease, but he kept his hands to himself as he nodded. "Okay then, I'll do the French toast."

Having completed the coffee making, Annie stood back enough to watch him as the firm bread was dipped into the egg, milk, and cinnamon mixture. She moved to warm maple syrup in a small pitcher and within minutes they were taking delight in the sweet breakfast treat and hot black coffee.

"Today," Shane began, "I have the end of a project to finish, maybe an hour's worth. After that, how about a ride? Being the Sunday after Thanksgiving, the stores are probably going to be busy in town, but we could head for smaller mom and pop shops toward the Cape. And soon, a day or two up north, a Christmas gift to us, and to Sherlock, of course."

Annie took a visible deep breath. "I'm excited for this season. The shopping today will be such fun, and the trip up north, I can barely wait."

Shane looked at her with his cup halfway between its saucer and his lips. She was genuinely happy and that meant the world to him. No one had ever taught him to love before in this manner; he liked the person he had become.

Sherlock finished his bowl of food and whined at the door to go out. "I'll take him," Shane said as he stood and walked to the back door. With the leash snapped in place, Shane stepped outside without a coat and shivered. Sherlock was urged to be quick and he was, then back into the warm house. Annie smiled at the two of them, both advocates of joy.

Wearing jeans and a dark green sweater beneath a warm jacket, Annie appeared in the living room where Shane waited with Sherlock at his side.

Shane observed her head to toe and smiled. "You look like a classy advertisement for winter attire, very nice."

Annie bowed as she had hundreds of times after a performance and then she smiled.

Shane was always entranced with her beauty, yet now he wondered if this stylish black jacket was one of many other garments which had been Albert's choice for her.

Annie slipped her hands into deep, warm pockets and thought about how much she loved this jacket, one of the first items of clothing she'd purchased for herself after Albert's death. In fact, she had nothing left of the New York wardrobe. Every item in her closet was from her choice, her funds.

Albert's choice or Annie's, Shane adored her – how could an item of clothing hold importance when measured against love? They walked to the car and, once belted securely, made their way through town and south toward the Cape.

Pale blue skies were dotted with peach-colored

clouds. Oaks, maples, and beech trees scattered their leaves to the wind, revealing stark branches as squirrels ran with their bounty for home. Annie loved the scenery, simple and ordinary to most.

Shane gave Sherlock a quick glance and smiled at the dog taking up the entire back seat. He then turned to Annie's flawless profile and felt his heart melting. He wanted to ask her about Albert, he wanted to know what she knew about the life he'd left behind in Austria. It wasn't the right time – this day was reserved for Christmas shopping and joy, no room for doubts and deceit.

The first shop they encountered had everything from collectibles to antiques and clothing to toys. For the women's shelter, Annie purchased several pairs of mittens for children and adults, warm socks, and small packages of candy. Shane found a stuffed penguin dog toy for Sherlock and two compatible scarves for Annie and himself. With purchases paid for, they left the store and walked diagonally across the street to a tea shop where Annie placed an order while Shane walked Sherlock. Back in the car, Sherlock was the recipient of a hotdog in a plain roll while Annie and Shane enjoyed hot coffee and a sandwich in a shop where they could keep a watchful eye on the car. Bright and sunny, the day was enjoyable beyond expectations.

"Will you wrap all those things you bought," Shane asked as they drove from the small Cape village, "or will you just drop them off as they are?"

"We'll wrap them," Annie said, and then she looked at Shane and smiled.

"We'll wrap them, as in *we*?"

Annie laughed and nodded her head. "That's what I mean."

Chapter Eighteen

Halfway between Thanksgiving and Christmas Annie stood at her kitchen sink one cold morning and looked out at Daisy's grave. Before snow, she wanted to put something there, something to keep the little cat's memory alive, sweetly recalled. She thought about what to place there, something taller than the eventual snow could conceal.

Shane walked into the kitchen and observed her thoughtful state of mind. With a hand gently to her shoulder he asked, "You okay?"

Annie turned to him for a moment and explained.

Shane looked out to the burial spot and then to Annie. "How about a little cross? I could make one with a couple of branches and a nail or two. We could sink it in the ground before we get a deep freeze. Would that do?"

Annie could feel tears forming in her eyes and she left them there, unashamed of feelings for the little cat who had welcomed her to Salt Hill Bay. "Yes," she said, "that would be perfect; something tall enough to defy the snow, yet simple enough to represent Daisy."

Shane fashioned a two-foot high cross from beech tree branches and prodded it into the firm ground.

Annie stood at his side, clutching a jacket to her chest as she reached down to rearrange a few stones and shells on the grave. As she stood, Shane reached for her arm

168

and then his hand slid over hers.

"You know what?" he said. "I think we need some nice, warm coffee and then we hit the road."

Annie looked at him with questions in her eyes.

"It's cold but beautiful. Let's pack up our pup here and head north."

"What about your work? It's Wednesday; don't you have reports due for Friday?"

Shane nodded as he tugged her into the cozy kitchen. "The Friday reports are my demands on myself, not the company's. When you're the boss of yourself, you need a little discipline – I make rules to follow. Friday reports are one of those rules. I think we need that trip up north: New Hampshire, Vermont, Maine, your choice. Let's have some more coffee and pack a few things to take, including food and bowls for our buddy here." He reached down to pet Sherlock then moved to the microwave where he heated two cups of coffee left over from breakfast.

Annie could feel the adrenalin slither through her system – the thought of going away was exciting. She accepted a steaming cup from Shane and thought about not having left this cottage overnight since she'd moved there. She loved this place, yet it would be wonderful to see the mountains, the meadows with frost, the open space of Northern New England. "Are we really doing this?"

Shane nodded. "As long as you're a willing captive."

"I need to go into your room," she said. "My overnight bag is on the shelf of your closet."

Shane felt a shock-wave go through his body. The boxes; had he placed them back as they'd been stored? "I'll get it for you," he said.

As Annie finished her coffee, Shane went to his room

and returned with a small piece of luggage. "Is this what you wanted?"

Annie reached for the small blue bag. "Yes, this will be fine. Are you all set for packing? I have other bags in the attic space."

Hearing the words attic space sent a chill through Shane. Were there more of Albert's possessions stored above the ceiling?

"I think I'm good. I have a few larger cases and one small duffle type bag – I'll use that. But where's the attic? What's up there?"

Annie set her lips in a very firm stance. "Just a dead body or two."

The stunned look on Shane's face made Annie bend over with laughter. "There's a pull-down stairs in my bedroom with access to a crawl space. All I have up there are a few pieces of luggage and a box of Christmas garlands I never remember to use. No dead things, I promise."

Shane looked at her with raised eyebrows. "Okay then, I'll pack a few warm sweaters and stuff. You pack for you, and we'll grab Sherlock's bowls and his favorite blanket. I'm ready for this adventure. Where would you like to go?"

"Vermont," she answered without hesitation.

~

Annie marveled at the change of scenery after the drive through Boston; just a few miles out of the city the terrain was pleasantly different from the southern coast of Massachusetts. Dotted with boulders, meadows, and gently rolling hills, she felt excited for what lay in store further north.

Shane glanced at her profile every little while and smiled – this had been a good decision, a spontaneous journey.

Sherlock, too, found it necessary every twenty or thirty miles to sit up from his backseat bed to take a look at the pastoral offerings.

"Interested in picking up a coffee?" he asked. "We could pull off the highway at the next exit, or we can go on; your choice."

Annie sat up straight, noting they had just entered New Hampshire. Vermont would be another hour or more. "Coffee sounds great."

They turned off at an exit for coffee and other amenities, plus a chance for Annie to walk Sherlock. Shane returned to the car with two coffees and a small variety of doughnuts, one plain for Sherlock. Within twenty minutes, they were back on the road heading north to their destination.

"Do we know where we're going?" Annie asked with a little laugh in her voice. "We never discussed anything other than Vermont."

Shane nodded as he drove. "That's true. I had a place in mind. There's a town just over the border, Quechee. Have you heard of it?"

Annie shook her head no.

Shane smiled at her enthusiastic expression. "Well, it's a pretty neat place. There's a gorge there, well-known, and it's picturesque, right in the middle of mountains, streams, and winding roads. I think you'll like it."

"I'm sure I will."

They drove in silence for several miles when Annie asked, "Have you been to this place, Quechee, before?"

"Yes, before I found Salt Hill Bay. I love New England; there's a fantastic variety of land here. In the end, I decided I would probably do better by the sea than in the mountains, especially during the winter. That was before you engineered taking care of my injuries. I can't believe the difference in my life since I had my body repaired. I owe it all to you."

Annie turned to look again at the bare branches, the revealed meadows. She thought about the cloistered life she'd led in New York; Albert had not been interested in leaving his home except for a theatre event, an opening show. This exploration of other places was new and exciting. Every inch of landscape was worthy of notice as it took her further from home and thoughts of missing Daisy. That, she knew, had been the reason for Shane's sudden suggestion to go north; he understood that Annie needed a sweet distraction.

"There's a big antique and craft center in Quechee. Maybe we'll find some great Christmas gifts there; more of those blue and white dishes for you?"

Annie smiled. "Maybe. I wouldn't mind a few more cups and saucers in case we invite guests over, and a serving plate would be nice."

Shane didn't inquire who they would ask to join them in the small cottage, but he liked the idea that Annie was interested in entertaining.

"Aren't you going to ask who we'd have over for dinner or dessert?"

Shane felt jarred, as if she'd read his mind. He glanced at her as he spoke. "I guess I'd be curious. Who did you have in mind?"

Annie laughed. "No one really; I used to think of who I'd invite, had it been my choice, when I lived in New York. Those who came were Albert's friends. He told me once that I could ask a friend over, but when I actually thought to invite her, he told me that with her being a lesser dancer than I was, it might be awkward. She and I were friends; I think it would have been fun, but Albert thought otherwise."

Shane was quiet. He was beginning to dislike Albert even more than when he'd discovered the letters. The man took this beautiful woman's years and talent to use for his own enrichment. Nothing about him seemed fair.

As thoughts continued for each of them, keeping their words silent, they arrived in Quechee, a three-hour journey from Salt Hill Bay. Annie felt a tinge of adrenalin race through her abdomen – a fluttering of joy for a world she was about to explore.

Shane pulled into a motor lodge and was told at the office that all rooms were taken. There was a festival in town that weekend to start the celebrations for Christmas, drawing visitors from across the country. At each of the next three stops they were told the same until the fifth try. At the Silver Shadows Lodge there was one room with one bed. Annie took a deep breath then agreed that they'd better take this available source.

"You'll love this room," the woman behind the office counter said with a welcoming smile. "There's a fireplace and the bed is king size, guaranteed to give you a good night's sleep."

Annie controlled a shiver running through her body and doubted she'd have that good night's sleep.

Shane refrained from smiling – his sideways glance at Annie told him to be still, to handle this like a grown-up. What he knew was that this woman he loved was bound to be anxious while he was determined to be understanding. He had not brought her to Vermont with seduction in mind.

Sherlock in tow, they went to their room, carrying with them their belongings from the car. As promised, the room was perfect.

Annie unpacked an outfit for the next day, hanging it in a closet. She then selected a two-piece outfit she would wear to bed, not the nightdress she had planned.

"We should go out in search of a bite to eat," Shane said. "There seem to be choices along this route. Anything you're wishing for?" As he spoke, he filled a water bowl for Sherlock and emptied a can of food into a dish.

"Will we be taking our boy?"

Shane smiled. "Yes, I think we will. He'd probably be afraid we'd abandoned him if we left him here alone. We'll find a place where we can see the car from the restaurant – he'll like that."

Annie nodded as she combed her long hair and announced she was ready to go.

The late afternoon drive through the hills and twisting roads was enchanting, revealing sloping fields and infinite stone walls. Annie could not take her eyes from her side of the road, amazed at the diversity of land. Flat, sea-kissed beaches at Salt Hill Bay were in sharp contrast to slopes dotted with sheep and trees, streams bubbling and intertwining among and over rocks.

"How about this?" Shane asked as they slowed near an Italian Bistro offering an extensive menu on an outdoor sign.

Annie agreed – they had something for every palate. Shane left the car running as he walked into the establishment to inquire about window seating, explaining the need to see Sherlock. Happily they accommodated the attractive pair with a cozy booth and a direct line of vision to their car and an anxious dog. Annie smiled as she noted that Sherlock was in the driver's seat, staring at the pair of humans he so loved.

After dinner and a brief stop to accrue snacks and a

174

bottle of Pinot Grigio, the threesome made their way back to the hotel. Shane and Annie walked Sherlock back into their room. The hearth became brilliant with warmth in minutes as Sherlock settled before the blaze, his dark eyes enchanted with the flickering light.

Shane opened the wine, secured two glasses, then emptied a bag of chips and a few apples into a large bowl on a coffee table before the small sofa. He invited Annie to sit. She looked at the fire without glancing at Shane.

"It's cozy here. I think I'll change so that when I feel really weary, I'll be able to slip into bed."

Shane nodded. "Sounds like a good move. I'll do the same shortly."

Shane poured wine and reached for a handful of spicy chips. When Annie walked into the room, he almost spilled his wine. Her pale hair was loose around her shoulders and she was wearing a pale lavender set of clothes, similar to yoga gear, tight-fitting jersey material on her slender form. She looked like a teen and yet relaxed with her womanhood.

She sat down inches away from him and reached for her glass. Her eyes on the hearth, she leaned back and found herself feeling more relaxed than she'd felt in years.

Later was a test for each of them. Annie climbed beneath the covers first, keeping toward the edge of the bed. Shane changed into leisure clothing and was careful when moving toward her – gentle maneuvers, no tugging at blankets. He was going to handle this right; no arm around her waist, no kiss to the beautiful lips. Just sleep. Sherlock settled on the sofa.

With morning light, Annie was on her right side facing the wall. She opened her eyes and was still, feeling weight across her waist. She stirred a bit and realized when he did that Shane's arm was draped across her body, his forehead pressed into the shallow dip between her shoulder blades.

Abruptly he moved and apologized. "Oh, sorry, Annie; I didn't mean to…"

"It's okay," she said as she moved her feet to the floor and then stood.

Shane quickly took Sherlock for a brief walk outside. When he returned, he found Annie's hair back in a ponytail and her bed clothing swapped for warmer garments. He showered and changed while Sherlock had breakfast, then they were off driving into a low morning bank of clouds as sunshine insisted itself through.

They stopped first for breakfast, then for shopping at a center filled with antiques, new clothing, and jewelry. Separating to shop for one another's Christmas gifts and not to leave Sherlock on his own in the car, Annie found a large copper ladle for Shane while he found a flow blue and white teapot for Annie. Wandering the antique section, she also found a creamer and sugar set and four small dessert plates. Satisfied with their chosen items, they concluded their shopping excursion.

"And now," Shane began as they sat in the car and he started the engine, "I'll show you the gorge and the surrounding area. It's quaint yet basic; I think you'll like the scenery. Then we'll need to decide if we're staying another night or going back to Salt Hill. We can figure that out later, after lunch."

Annie took a deep breath and smiled. "This must be pretty close to Heaven."

Shane smiled at her sweet profile. She seemed fragile, like a piece of Dresden china. "You probably thought the same thing when you found Salt Hill Bay," he said.

Annie shook her head. "No, not really; I just

176

appreciated the change. I've come to love Salt Hill Bay; it's home, but at first it was simply the stark difference, away from city life."

The declaration from Annie surprised Shane. Had she been so desperate to escape New York and the ghostly memories of all she'd encountered there?

They dined in a quaint post and beam restaurant, again facing windows from the inside so that Sherlock could see them and they could see him. Shane ordered a piece of roasted chicken for the waiting dog, who actually consumed his food before Annie and Shane had theirs.

After a ride along twisting roads through mountains and a stop for gas, the decision was made to head home, three hours back to Salt Hill. They went back to Silver Shadows, retrieved their things, and checked out. They vowed to return again in spring, to stay longer and explore further.

Annie's eyes sought every branch, every bird along the way. This had been the adjustment she had been seeking: the hope that more was waiting than the limitations her life had held until Shane. He had become the integral part she longed for: the connection, the exploring, the love.

Walking through the front door of the cottage, each of them felt the comfort of being back at home. Sherlock, too, seemed joyful as he pranced into the living room and onto the sofa.

"I feel like we've been away for days," Annie said with a smile to Shane. "There's so much to see in a place as beautiful as Vermont; it's easy to be fooled by how long we were there."

"We'll go again whenever you wish. Spring will be nice there, autumn will be fantastic. We'll make it our place to visit; there's lots more to explore."

It was dark as they placed clothing away and fed Sherlock. Annie made coffee and they talked about what, if anything, they wanted for dinner. They had settled into a comfortable routine together, appreciating their simple little home by the sea.

~

It was after Christmas and the stringent winter snows when Annie began to work once again with the women and children at the shelter. The needs there were endless for more than tangible items like clothes. It seemed closer, Annie thought, to being a stage dancer than anything else she encountered. These women had no choices. Their lives were determined by unfortunate relationships and poverty. Dancers, because they danced, because they lived among the lights, did not understand that they, too, could be poor.

It was what seemed to Shane to be a sudden decision when Annie arrived at his bedroom door late one night. She said nothing as she slipped out of a robe, revealing a sheer, knee-length nightdress in pale blue. Shane was startled, not sure that she wasn't ill.

"Everything okay?" he asked as he half sat up in bed.

Annie moved slowly toward him without a reply. She pulled the covers aside and placed her body as close to him as physically possible.

With morning light, Shane turned toward where Annie had been. The slight lavender scent was there in her place and he wondered if it had been a dream. That tender interlude had been his hope for years.

He dressed and went into the kitchen where he found fresh coffee. He looked around the corner to the small living room and found Annie sitting there, enjoying a fire in the hearth, Sherlock at her feet. With a cup in his hand, he joined her, sitting across from her in a chair.

"Are you okay?"

Annie looked from the hearth to Shane. "I'm fine, but we need to talk."

Shane's heart sank. Was she going to explain her regrets about last night and tell him to go?

"Okay," he said as he stiffened and sat back further into the chair.

Annie balanced her coffee cup and saucer on her lap as she turned to face him squarely. "We're more this morning to one another than we were yesterday at this time."

Shane nodded, his eyes fastened to hers.

"No one, until you, has known me. I want to tell you who I am. I don't want concealments to stand between us."

Again, Shane was silent as he took a swallow of coffee then placed the cup down on a table next to the chair.

Annie rubbed her eyes and looked at the hearth. She turned abruptly and looked at Shane. "Last night, in your room, was wonderful. It was also a reminder of the months after Albert's death. I have two cardboard boxes on the shelf of your closet. They contain letters from Albert's mother in Austria."

Shane swallowed, wondering if she had detected his exploration of those boxes and was now going to tell him that it had been a despicable act on his part.

"Albert kept them in a concealed space beneath a stairway in the New York house. I'm sure he thought I'd never see them. The housekeeper found them and gave them to me. I had no idea they existed – they opened a world once disguised."

Shane shifted in his chair. She hadn't known of Albert's former life – a partner, a son.

179

"Those cartons are the reason I sold the New York house and moved here. They changed everything." She hesitated, looking near tears, but shedding no moisture from her fetching eyes. She looked from the rug directly at Shane.

Shane sat forward, intent on her divulging this intricate part of her life, a part that surely must have destroyed her confidence in her husband, if not all others.

"I'm not sure how much I want to talk about this right now. I thought I could." She stood up and walked toward the hearth. Her eyes caressed the shells on the mantle and then she turned to look at Shane. "Last night," she began, "I needed you. I needed to feel close to you, Shane."

Shane stood and walked to her, longing to touch her. He moved his hands into his trouser pockets and looked at the torture reflected on her face. "You know that I love you, Annie. Last night was wonderful."

Annie moved away from him and back to her seat on the sofa. She nodded but was silent.

Shane moved to sit across from her again. "This life we share, it's so much more than I ever thought I'd know. This little house, this huge dog, our whispered way of living; it's perfect. At least it is for me; I'm hoping it is for you, too."

Annie reached for her coffee cup, a trace of a smile on her lips. "We have something very special."

Shane was silent as he breathed a sigh of relief. He sat back and reached for his own coffee, taking a long swallow. At some point, he knew, he would have to be honest with her about the boxes filled with letters – he owed her a genuine partner.

Chapter Nineteen

In the days and weeks that followed, with spring on their doorstep and jonquils daring to rise from cold ground, Shane thought often of the boxes on his shelf. Every night Annie made herself comfortable in his bed, or he in hers, her head often pressed to his heart, her arm possessively draped across his abdomen. This was what he wanted and couldn't bear to lose.

In a day of brilliant sunshine and after a walk through town with Annie on his right, Sherlock to his left, they stopped for coffee and sat outside to enjoy the day and the friendly amblers who wandered by. He couldn't wait any longer to take the risk of telling her what he knew. He would, however, wait until they were settled back at home.

Annie took in the architecture indicative of colonial times. She recalled her first impression of New York when she began to dance there as a child. She had cherished her meadows and brooks at the family farm, yet in the radiance of New York, she found another dimension in the sky-scrapers, the brownstones, the mix of modern with ancient. Living in Salt Hill Bay had managed to combine her worlds – the quiet of her own little neighborhood on the fringe of town, and the town itself, bustling with tourists and common people living their lives.

She thought often about approaching the subject of the boxes again, their content and her feelings. Shane had every right to know what made her who she was, that is, if she could comprehend each transition she'd made. This one, this life with Shane seemed more valid and true than any other.

"Should we head back?" Shane questioned softly as he stood, securing Sherlock's leash in his hand.

Annie rose, her coffee cup in her right hand, her left hand extended to Shane.

While their ten-minute walk back to the cottage was in silence, each with their own thoughts, Shane was first to speak after their coats were hung in a closet and Sherlock's leash was unfastened.

He sat down across from the sofa, rubbed his face with both hands, then looked at Annie. "If you haven't something planned, I'd like to talk to you for a bit. Were you planning on time at the shelter today?"

"I can go anytime. We can talk." Annie settled back onto the sofa, one leg folded under her body.

Shane rubbed his chin, looked at the mantle, then back at Annie's face.

She was focused, aware that Shane had something on his mind. In her trembling heart, she hoped it was not that he was once again preparing to leave. There had been an informal thread of comings and goings in her life. Each time worsened, especially with Shane.

He cleared his throat and swallowed. "The boxes. I'd like to talk about the boxes on my closet shelf."

"Do you want me to tell you about the letters? I mean, I can do that if you want me to. I tried before; I just couldn't handle it at that time. I think I could now."

Shane looked at the stunningly winsome face of the woman he loved. "It's more what I need to say, Annie."

182

She shifted in her seat, moving the leg beneath her, feet to the floor, knee to knee. The strength in her body feeling wilted.

"Annie, I had a night when I couldn't sleep. I paced my room, I sat, I stood, and I ended up going to the closet."

Annie took a deep breath, apprehensive about what words would follow.

"I lifted the boxes onto my bed. I know I had no right, but I looked at the contents. I found the letters."

Annie felt her mouth go dry. "Did you read any of them?"

Shane nodded. "A few."

They were both silent as those words were digested and accepted.

"I had no right, Annie. I thought I'd find at the most some of your husband's old clothing: gloves, a hat. I was pretty surprised to find letter after letter, all from the same address."

"And you read them."

Shane nodded again. "Yes, a few of them."

Annie stood and walked around the room then back toward where Shane sat. "I need a coffee. Would you like some?"

"Yes, I would love a coffee."

Annie left the room long enough to heat two cups of coffee and then she returned, handing one to Shane. She sat down and looked at him, waiting for him to continue.

Shane stared into the black brew, took a sip, then looked at Annie. "I'm sorry, Annie. I shouldn't have violated your privacy; I had no right."

Annie looked from his face to the sunshine still lingering outside. When she looked back at him she asked, "What did you discover by reading the letters from Albert's mother?"

Shane felt his abdomen quiver. "He had a son."

Annie steadied her eyes on Shane's. She was silent.

Shane looked at her serene face and knew that this was not new information to her; for that, he was glad. "You knew."

Annie's lips flexed slightly before she replied. "I knew through the same source, Shane: the letters. It wasn't something Albert shared."

Shane wanted to cry for her, for the deception which made her a victim. He wasn't sure how to continue.

"Did you find the letter from Albert to his mother?"

Shane hesitated. "Yes, I did."

Annie sipped her coffee, seeming more composed than she had been.

"It actually feels good to know that you know. I could not divulge to Albert's friends what I discovered. I did not think my family would understand. I kept it all inside. To explain the letter from Albert, his mother gave it to me, to demonstrate her son's *devotion* to me, to my ability in dance."

Shane frowned and sat forward. "She *gave* it to you? Did she come for her son's funeral?"

Annie's wry smile was accompanied with her explanation. "No. His orders were that she was not to know he was ill, she was not to know he was gone until it was over. After I read the contents of the boxes, I went to Austria."

Shane felt unsettled. He had envisioned Annie as a frail weeping widow in need of support. He had been wrong; she was fortified with determination to discover exactly the depth of lies she had been living.

"I knocked on her door and she immediately knew who I was. She invited me in for tea. She told me that,

184

from Albert's description, she would know me anywhere, and she gave me a letter he had written to her. You read that letter. It tells of his admiration for my dancing, and how I had brought attention to him as a famous conductor – there was no mention of love."

Shane felt moisture filling his eyes. He looked away, brushed threatening tears from his face, then looked back at Annie.

"I'm okay, Shane."

He thought about joining her on the sofa but resisted, allowing her space and time to adjust and continue if she chose to. "Did you meet his son?"

Annie looked into the darkness of her coffee and then to the windows where the light of day was fading. "He had died, just two weeks after Albert."

"Oh, my God," Shane whispered. "How ironic."

"His mother explained to me why I never had a child with Albert. He was afraid we'd have another like his son, genetically damaged. It turned out that the mother, a woman Albert had not married, was the one carrying the damaging genes. Until the boy died at the age of nearly thirty, no one knew the fact that the issue had come from his mother's side."

Shane sat melded to the chair in which he sat. Through the dozen plus years he had known and loved Annie, he thought of her as vulnerable, fragile. She was anything but delicate and insecure. She had traveled to Austria after her husband's loss, not content to allow further untruths.

"What did you say to her? Did the news of his death come from you?"

Annie shook her head. "No. After his burial, Albert's secretary, a man, sent his mother a message and a fair amount of funds, as directed by Albert. Everything he

185

did was orchestrated, his entire life."

"So you went to Austria to see his mother and son?"

Annie looked around the room and then back at Shane. "I went to see them, yes, but I also went to confirm in my mind what had happened to me in those twenty-three years of marriage. Why I had been so believing; I needed to understand. I also went to deliver the remainder of Albert's wealth. I didn't want it. I had my own money from dancing to buy this cottage, to live out my life modestly. And here I am."

They were both quiet for several minutes, each of them analyzing their own thoughts.

"Annie," Shane began, "I'm sorry. You deserved so much more."

"Anyone would deserve more. Everyone deserves truth in their life. Sometimes I feel numb when I think of those years with Albert. He had what he wanted, which was a shallow sense of fame, I helped him to achieve. He was absent from his own mother and child and, for me, there was a shadowy nothingness. I was very angry at first, and then I decided that Albert had taken enough of me. I was going to live here by the sea and immerse myself in the serene offerings of the land. I was not going to let another person into my space. Until you." Annie smiled at Shane's handsome face, a face revealing concern and sadness.

"I'm okay, Shane, really, I'm okay."

At that point, he moved from his chair, stepped over the dog, and sat down next to Annie. He wrapped his arms and emotions around her, holding her close without the need for words.

They sat together for nearly an hour before Annie gently shifted her body to stand. They went into the kitchen where Sherlock was fed, then each of them sliced vegetables for salad and a hearty bread they would warm in the oven. The entire evening was strewn with simple tasks, watching TV, and being together. That night in bed was all consuming, like nothing either of them had known before. There were no barriers to hurdle; they loved and they slept soundly.

Annie seemed more lighthearted for days after their revealing conversation. She went to the shelter and taught dance moves to the women and children; she sorted through donated clothing. She came back to the cottage each day renewed, prepared to be whole, to feel the wonder of contented love.

On one such day, Shane, after working for hours, took a break to prepare chili for dinner. Annie walked into the house and commented on the tantalizing aroma, and then she staggered as she slipped out of her jacket.

Shane reached out to her, concerned for the pale skin on her beautiful face. "Hey," he said, "what just happened? Are you okay?"

"Sure," she answered, "just a little tired."

"Annie," he began as he gripped her slim shoulders, "it's more than that. What's going on?"

She slipped her shoes off and sat in a kitchen chair. "I'll be fine. I just had a little twinge of something in my stomach. I'm okay."

That night, beneath the covers of the bed in Annie's room, they huddled close together. Shane closed his eyes as he pressed the right side of his face to her left shoulder. Before they slept, he thought about the source of Annie's pain, the result of dancing, torturing her legs and feet into submission. He felt angry with Albert for what he took from Annie besides the years in which he persuaded her to wear herself thin. Now this illness, all because her limbs were aching and she sought relief through seemingly harmless medications.

A trip to her doctor in the days ahead proved that it was more than fatigue. Annie's liver was still not fully mended. She took the news in stride, knowing that something within her abdominal area was amiss. Shane was concerned.

On a glorious spring morning, with sun filling every crack and crevice it could reach, Annie and Shane walked through town, Sherlock half prancing at their sides. They stopped to buy coffee and muffins then headed back to the cottage. Inside, Annie shed her light jacket and opened the windows to let in the fresh air. Shane unhooked Sherlock's leash and hung his and Annie's jackets in the entryway closet.

"Annie," he began, "we need to talk."

Annie's throat constricted, fear spilled through her core, and she closed her eyes momentarily. She turned to face him, waiting.

"Let's sit down with our coffee and muffins," he said. "We can talk in between bites and swallows."

Annie moved like a dancer, each step deliberate, toward the sofa where Sherlock had curled himself up into a large ball. Shane handed her the paper cup of hot coffee, placed the muffins before both of them on the trunk, then looked at her pale blue eyes.

"We need to get married," he said.

Annie didn't know whether to laugh or cry. She had feared being told that he was once again going away – marriage was the last thing on her mind.

With her silence, Shane continued. "We are more than two people who love one another. We depend on each other. If I had an injury, or you were to need hospital care, there are limitations when the patient is not related to the visitor or caretaker. You know how that works,

Annie. It's the privacy factor; it keeps people apart when they're in intensive care, unless they're related. We need to fix this, Annie, so that no one and nothing can keep us apart."

Annie sat still, aware that he was right, yet recalling the promise she made to herself with the purchase of her cottage: no commitments to anyone from that day on.

Shane looked at Annie's relaxed expression, her eyes moving from him to the windows, then back at his concerned face.

"Annie? Do you agree?"

Annie took a deep breath. "I understand what you're saying," she began as she moved strands of pale hair away from her face. "Really, I do understand, Shane. It's just that…"

"What? What keeps us from getting married, Annie? We love each other. If something should happen to either of us, something serious, we'd want to be together, wouldn't we?"

Annie stood and walked around the room then returned to the sofa, her right leg nestled beneath her body. She looked at Shane and lightly bit her lower lip. "I love you, Shane. I tried not to, but here I am. I agree with what you've said, that in an emergency, one of us incapacitated, the other would be needed. Couldn't we draw up a contract of sorts, one that gives the other of us permission to make decisions?"

Shane looked down then right back up into her eyes. "Annie, is there a reason you wouldn't want to be married to me?"

Annie's eyes filled with tears and spilled onto her hands.

Shane moved to the sofa, squeezing into a small space between Annie and Sherlock. "Hey," he said as he

189

wrapped his arms around her, "where's the bad part of us being hitched? We're as together as any two people could be. It's just a certificate, one that would guarantee no one could part us. Please, Annie, marry me." He reached into his pocket and pulled out a small box. Inside was a demure ring he'd purchased at an antique shop downtown. He'd chosen it because it reminded him of his Annie: understated and simply perfect.

Reaching for a tissue through tears, Annie murmured, "Okay."

The spring wedding was held in the garden on a sun-filled day; a justice of the peace performed the ceremony, Sherlock in attendance. Annie wore a pale pink gauze dress to her bare feet. Shane wore a grey suit and tie, shoes on, and Sherlock wore a blue scarf around his neck. With the ceremony final, gold bands on the ring fingers of both Shane and Annie, they laughed at what they had done with spontaneity and pure joy. They celebrated with white wine, strawberries, and brie, and two small treats for their beloved dog.

"Now," Shane teased later, his arms filled with Annie, "I have the legitimate right to ravage you, night after night, day after day."

"Now just a minute," she said, laughing and pushing him to arms' length, "have I no say in this?"

"Sure," he said, "you have every right to ravage me as well, any time you want."

Annie collapsed into his arms with laughter and kisses. After several close moments, she pushed away from him and looked into his eyes, her own brimming with undeniable love. "I may take you up on that offer more than you'd anticipated," she said.

"Any time," he responded as he held her close, his heart bursting with joy to call this woman his wife.

"Guess what?" he began as he caressed her slim back through the thin fabric "We need a honeymoon. Would you like to choose a place, or would you want to do Vermont again? This time we could share the bed and give it a work-out."

Annie laughed. "Yes to Vermont," she replied, hugging him close.

"Great. I'll call Silver Shadows and ask for our room," he said with a wink.

Within days, they packed a few clothing items, their dog and his food, then drove north. The trip this time was relaxed; they knew one another well and each found a sense of security in the certificate binding them together.

As Shane drove the highway through New Hampshire, Annie recalled the day she and Albert had wed. There had been a designer gown, a champagne reception with more than four-hundred people, and the music was a collection of Albert's compositions. This marriage to Shane, this simple garden delight, filled with love and privacy was all that mattered. No photos to save the day, but memories of love where bruised hearts had endured aggrieved emotions.

"Annie," Shane said, easing his wife out of her thoughts. "We're here. Back to the very room with the fireplace and all, only this time, as wife and husband."

Annie laughed. "Now that's being politically correct if I ever heard it, putting the wife first. I like that. You're a very smart man."

Shane reached over to kiss her then backed away just enough to look at what was now his. Her beauty always astounded him, but more than that, he was impressed with her obvious strength when confronted with the information Albert had carefully concealed. She was small in stature, yet tall and strong in her convictions, true to herself in the way she chose to live when the choice had been hers. He respected his wife; he held admiration beyond anything he'd felt for anyone else in his life – this woman was a serene, ravishing bundle of charm, and he could scarcely believe his good fortune in having her solidly in his life. There would never be anyone other than Annie.

Shane took his eyes from her as he shut down the car's engine. He would set the hearth ablaze, he would pour some wine, and he would mingle their love with showing her parts of the state abloom with spring that she could only have imagined; meadows and hills wearing pink laurel and lavender, roadside daisies and Black-eyed Susans. His objective was to provide Annie with days of splendor and nights of bliss. Each of them had, through the decisions of others, misdirected lives prior to meeting on the beach – this was their time.

"What do you think," Shane asked as they lay in bed, the hearth ablaze. "If we'd met twenty years ago, would we have had a family?"

Annie's response was quick. "At least a dozen," she replied.

Shane laughed. "Hey, I'm not talking cupcakes here; a dozen might have been quite a challenge."

Annie laughed, her face aglow from the tangerine flames against the fieldstone. "Well, at least five."

"Why five?"

Annie snuggled closer to Shane. "I had five dolls."

Shane felt suddenly sad. So much of the child had been left in the Connecticut hills, her childhood interrupted by well-meaning parents and enthusiastic dance instructors. A young girl with dancing ability was whisked away and taught discipline in how she moved and how she lived. But they couldn't teach her to forget

192

what she'd loved about home.

"Five would have been fun," he said, giving her a light squeeze.

Annie sat up on one elbow and looked at his handsome face. "You could still be a father, Shane."

Shane looked into her eyes, saddened for what had not been part of her life, children and a normal home. "Annie, my purpose in life was never clear until I met you. Had we met younger, I'm sure we would have loved kids, but we didn't. I'm forty-four; at this age having a child would mean I'd be retiring about the time he or she graduated from high school, or definitely college. We have each other, and you, my darling, are far more than I ever thought of for a wife. When I think of what we have, I'm much more than grateful; I'm in awe. We have now. We have one another." He pulled her closer to him, her body willing to be pressed against his, close enough to be one.

After four days in Vermont, touring the back roads and haunting antique shops for copper and flow blue dishes, they decided it was time to go home. Sherlock, while enjoying his romps in a variety of woods and pastures, seemed a bit confused. He, too, would no doubt be glad to be in familiar surroundings inside the cottage near the salty sea.

Chapter Twenty

It was a warm morning when Shane saw from their kitchen window Annie sitting in the garden; she plucked weeds from the circle of stones and shells defining Daisy's grave. Her coffee mug was near to her and he smiled.

He heated a cup of coffee for himself then turned to look outside before joining her and Sherlock. He nearly dropped the mug as his eyes saw Annie's body stretched limply over a plant she would never have chosen to harm. He ran to her, placing his legs each side of her body, reaching down to her face, her neck with pleas for her to be okay.

She was still, unmoving; he was not sure that she was breathing. He placed his fingers to her neck, then to her wrist. There was a pulse. Without hesitation he ran into the house for his cell phone then back out to Annie. She came to as the emergency team placed her on a stretcher and prepared to take her to the area hospital.

Shane secured Sherlock in the house and then followed the ambulance as it carried the person he loved more than life itself. The process was swift, yet it seemed to take forever as emergency room nurses and doctors tended to the delicate woman before them. Tests were done and medical history taken. Annie's diagnosis was delivered to the two of them at her bedside; she was anemic as well as magnesium depleted. She had also been suffering silently with pain from the compromised liver.

"It will take time and rest," the doctor told Shane in a shadowy hallway. "She's frail. You'll have to make sure she eats and there will be supplements; magnesium, iron, and generally good nutrition should help. I don't want to frighten you, but this is serious. Your wife is going to need your full attention."

Shane swallowed and felt like he'd sob if he was alone. "Is she going to be all right? Please don't tell me I could lose her."

The doctor reached out to momentarily touch Shane's shoulder. "Annie is fragile. We'll do our best to make her stronger, but it's going to fall on you to make sure she eats and does not over exert. This condition makes her vulnerable. Take good care of her, Mr. Bellows."

The doctor left him alone outside Annie's hospital room. Shane took a deep breath before going to her bedside with agony in his heart and a smile on his lips. She seemed small, defenseless, and weak. It frightened him to think of her condition and the years he'd hoped were a promising rather than precarious future. He could not imagine a life without her.

Annie smiled and reached for his hand. "Don't look so concerned," she said. "I see those eyes behind the smile. I'll be okay, Shane. I was told I must eat. I do eat, but I am going to be diligent about our meals – we're both going to be fine."

Shane swallowed back tears and gripped her hand in both of his. "I'm going to make you pancakes when I get you home," he said. "I know you like them, and we'll have strawberries and blueberries with them, and real maple syrup we bought in Vermont."

Annie squeezed his hands and smiled. "And I will happily eat them," she said.

Released after several days, Annie was excited to be home with Sherlock who was exhibiting his joy with her presence. His tail wagged side to side in a rhythm which managed to move his hind quarters as Annie and Shane laughed.

"I am so thankful to be home," she said as Shane walked with her to the sofa.

"Would you prefer bed, or are you okay here?"

Annie looked up at him. "I'm fine. It's just seemed like a long six days in the hospital, but this is my haven: you, Sherlock, and this humble abode."

"How about some tea? I picked up your favorite muffins, too, and I have fruit of all kinds. What interests you?"

Annie was quick to reply, "Tea and one of those muffins. I'll have the good-for-me fruit later."

Shane leaned forward and kissed her lightly. He left Sherlock adoringly at her feet while he went to the kitchen to make tea. Standing at the sink, he looked out to the garden, reliving finding her there, seemingly lifeless. Tears formed in his eyes and he whisked them away as he ran water and dug out her pretty blue and white dishes in which to serve her food.

Shane believed he'd been given a gift in Annie and had not thought for a moment he'd neglected her, but he was taking the doctor's words to heart; he would take care of her with every particle of his being; she would be well again.

Annie did not change the way she moved about in her treasured life. She found comfort in the garden with Sherlock at her side as Shane worked. They lessened their walks in town and on the beach so that mornings were quiet and restful while early evenings became time to slowly walk and take in the details of the town and the sea. Annie continued to reach for the pretty stones, the scallop shells, and the occasional, treasured sea glass.

"Isn't it renewing to have this closeness with the sea?" she asked as they walked on the shore. "Gardens and bodies of water: they're proof that life is meant to circulate and go on. And look at the lights in town," she said as she turned from the beach to the shoreline. "I love looking at the shops and houses with their lights aglow. They look like they're living, inviting us back."

Shane squeezed her hand as they walked, enchanted with his wife's observations. More than once he wondered what would have happened to her had he not returned from New Mexico. She had saved him years earlier from a life of incapacitating pain, and now it was his turn to take care of her in the most thorough and tender manner possible.

Shane's eyes examined her face and then the lights of town. He smiled at her and pulled her closer to his side. "We'll go home to our own little lights and a nice supper by the hearth. Summers by the sea can be chilly; I think we need a nice little fire while we have our lasagna and a good glass of wine."

Annie rested her forehead momentarily against Shane's shoulder then smiled up at him. "You color my life," she said. "Before you, nothing and no one had ever managed that. Thank you, Shane."

He stopped for a moment as they reached the layers of loose stones before the street. He adjusted Sherlock's leash in his hand and then scooped Annie up into his arms to carry her over the unstable rocks. She squealed and then laughed, not expecting the sudden motion. Within seconds, he planted her safely and gently on the town sidewalk to the applause of a few standers-by. Annie laughed again, happy to hold his hand as they walked toward home. She no longer thought about their difference in age. They were aligned in spirit.

Shane placed the blue and white dishes before Annie, serving amber tea, salad, and lasagna. "Did you know the town is having a bonfire on the beach July third? We could take blankets and Sherlock, and a good cup of coffee? Interested?"

Annie shifted back on the sofa, balancing the lasagna on her thighs. "I saw a poster at the café. Do you think we could take Sherlock?"

"Sure, we wouldn't desert our kid; he'll love it."

Annie cut into the delicious meal and took a bite. "You've become such a good cook. I don't think I served you this quality in food when you were recovering from surgery."

"You saved me," he said. "I was worn down, ready to give up. Those soups and hearty meals were energizing. That's my aim now, to get you strong."

They sat across from one another, casual conversation dotting their meal.

"I've made a decision," she said.

Shane looked up from taking a swallow of wine.

"Those cartons on your bedroom shelf are no longer welcome here. The poster for the bonfire stated that clean paper goods could be added to the fire. It's time for the letters to go."

Shane dabbed at his mouth with a napkin and stared at her. "Are you sure? Aren't they all you have left from your former marriage?"

Annie left her plate on the small trunk before her. "I never really had anything of Albert to keep. He was doing what he needed to exist. I understand that he used

198

me to interpret his music, his conducting, but it was all he knew to do. I'm not angry that he was insensitive to others' needs, even his own child's. Fame and money were his loves. Yes, I'm ready to let go."

It was at night in bed when each of them soundlessly visited their emotions. Shane watchfully guarded any change in Annie's condition; nothing mattered more than her well-being.

Annie lay in bed, Shane's arms wrapped around her, listening to his steady, strong breathing, feeling the motion of his body in rest. She prayed for time with him. Often her stomach ached and she said nothing. It reminded her that she needed to be grateful for every wonderful moment with her little family and cozy home. She had never aspired to be famous; fame could leave one in a lonely place. She'd never imagined a love as strong as what she had found in Salt Hill Bay. Tears sometimes slid from her eyes as she both appreciated and begged for more of the life she owned. There was a harmony, a oneness between them. Two weeks later they sat on the beach and watched as brilliant orange and gold flames turned cartons of letters into flakes of ash and then vapor. Shane reached for her hand, sandwiching it between his hand and his knee. He watched her face as she gazed upward at leaping flames; she was aglow with confidence and serenity.

Annie hugged her knees as she sat, her eyes watching the flames consume the remainder of Albert's existence. He'd been encouraging; he'd provided a beautiful home and opportunities she'd never expected. She was grateful. She thought of her journey to Austria, meeting the woman who had given Albert life. She had to have been in her eighties, stooped and small in stature, yet feisty and filled with pride for what her only child had accomplished in life. It didn't seem to matter that Albert had not returned to Austria, that he had not visited his own son. He had become prominent in the music and stage world of New York and beyond; that seemed to be the highlight of his mother's life.

Annie thought, too, of her own childhood and the family she'd been whisked away from at the age of eight. There was no one left at that Connecticut farm she cared to return to. Her mother's younger brother was living there now, a widower with no children; a lonely, bitter man who had turned to whiskey for comfort. It could, Annie decided, be distressful to return there for a visit, as beautiful as the area was. It felt as though the place itself had expelled her to a life far removed from wandering hills, lively brooks, and enchanting woodlands. She had missed it, until now, until Shane.

He hugged her, tempted to say something, but instead he watched her eyes, the way she seemed to approve of her past turning into sprinkles of ash disappearing into the night sky. Annie had taught him who she was; not a woman who defied life, but a stoic woman who gently took control of her beliefs. She was admirably confident.

When the fire began to dwindle and the crowd on the beach dispersed, Annie stood, brushed sand from her tan slacks, then reached down for Shane's hand.

He smiled as she offered to tug him up, this diminutive woman against his sturdy frame. He unfolded his legs from sitting and stood next to her, Sherlock at his side.

"I think we should go home and celebrate," he said. "We have that nice bottle of Pinot Grigio, or maybe you'd like the Merlot."

Annie laughed. "You know what I'd like? I'd like a cup of cocoa. Let's go."

Their walk home was thoughtful. Shane wrapped his large hand around hers, both fulfilled and terrified with this love of his life. He watched and worried continuously about her illness and what it had taken from her body and his heart. He could not lose her.

They had cocoa as Sherlock enjoyed a biscuit and fresh water. Each of them was muted with thought as they enjoyed the comfort of their sofa.

Shane thought to ask about regrets at turning those letters to ash, but he was quiet, deciding that Annie knew what she had done; there was no use revisiting the subject when the endeavor had been completed.

Annie was certain. The burning of the written words had freed her from giving more of herself to a life she had not chosen, and to a man who had loved her accomplishment in dance, her interpretive gestures on stage, but not her. Dancing had been playful to Annasheeva, not somber, but a game to see how much of the music she could ingest and pour out of herself for the audience to observe. She understood that the manner in which she heard the music, felt it flow through her veins, was unique, but she didn't care. The woman on stage was an imitation of Anne Snow, a little girl who had loved her home in the countryside, but was seldom allowed to return.

That night in bed, this time in Shane's room where those cartons of letters had been given a life now gone, Annie moved closer to Shane, so close that he knew she needed to be heart to heart, skin to skin. For Shane, it was the confirmation that no one could either arrest or cause hesitation to the love they shared. Completely, Annie was as much his as he was hers.

When she woke in the morning, she sat forward, leaning on her elbows as she glanced at Shane's boyish face. In his mid-forties, he was even more handsome than he had been when they'd met more than a dozen years before. She smiled at the slightly opened mouth, the full lips, and the peace reflected on his dear face.

She moved slowly so as not to wake him, pulling the covers aside, her feet on the floor. She made coffee and then slipped out to the garden where she plucked a few weeds and chose a withering rose to bring inside. While cutting melon and scrambling eggs for breakfast, Shane appeared at her side, rested his head against hers, his arms folded around her core.

"Should we have an argument once in a while?" she asked with the spatula in her hand and facing him.

Shane backed away a few inches and laughed. "What? Why? Why would we argue?"

Annie turned back to the eggs and stirred as she sprinkled pepper and salt into the mixture. "I thought couples argued once in a while."

"What would we argue about? Did you argue with Albert?"

Annie turned the burner off and prepared to shift the eggs from pan to plates. "No, never; but that's what I mean. Don't normal couples argue? With Albert, he made the decisions; there was nothing to bicker about."

Shane frowned then placed his hands each side of her radiant face to deliver a kiss. "I can't think of a single thing to argue with you about. If you find something, you let me know and I'll take Sherlock for a walk."

"Now or when I figure out something to squabble about?"

Shane smiled. "Either way; I'm not crazy about confrontations, but at the moment our boy here is looking like he might enjoy a quick trip outside."

Annie set the table with other items for their breakfast,

while Shane disappeared into the back gardens, returning to a table graced with a fresh yellow rose and an appetizing meal. He took note of her youthful ponytail reaching halfway down her slim back, the pale pink jersey she wore with a long, pearl gray skirt and no shoes. He wondered if the bare feet felt less pain against cool floors.

"I have an idea," she said, sitting back in her chair with her coffee in hand. "What would you think of us doing a little remodeling here?"

Shane looked at her, waiting for the concept to take form.

"We have two rather small bedrooms. What would you think of us taking down the wall between the two, creating a nice big walk in closet we could share, and having a wonderful master bedroom?"

Shane sat back and looked at her gleaming face. "You know, that's a great idea. It might be a load bearing wall, we'd need to add a hefty beam if that's the case, but we could have a contractor come in to do that part, and I could do the rest."

"And I could help," she said. "I know I could handle a paint brush. Then we would have no choices to make at bedtime, your room or mine. It would be ours."

"I'm in," Shane said as he stood and walked to her. "Come here, woman, I need to press my lips to yours."

Annie complied with the request, clinging to him as he twirled her around.

Within two months, as autumn approached, their room was complete, open and airy. The walls were painted a pale periwinkle blue and a white rug was centered beneath and around the new king-sized bed.

They stared at the finished space. "This," Shane began, "was a terrific idea."

Annie smiled. "It's ours. I wanted to make it completely ours. And soon, I want to talk to you about this humble little property and its ownership."

Shane nodded, willing to listen.

Annie left the room and walked toward the kitchen. "I'm so happy we did this together," she said as coffee was poured for two. "This is our home; o*ur* home. I want your name on the deed along with mine."

He didn't ask why, he didn't argue the point. Shane understood that Annie wanted the shared deed as he'd wanted their marriage, just in case.

"Okay," he said as he closed his eyes and hugged her close.

Annie lay in bed that night after Shane closed his eyes in sleep. She thought about her own demise for the first time, that her absence would matter. She did not want Shane to miss her in a manner that could cripple his life. Yet what she knew was that he would take care of Sherlock. He would tend to the little garden where Daisy was evident among the flowers, shells and stones. And she genuinely hoped that when life had expired for her, he would find someone new to love. Shane Bellows had restored her joy – she did not want his being to diminish as had hers after Albert's death.

When morning dawned with brilliant sunshine, she sighed, touching the empty space next to her and being drawn to the aroma of coffee wafting into their room. She felt grateful. Life in New York as a dancer had been disciplined joy, the movement energizing and playful. It had not been a grueling, terribly lonely existence. And marriage to Albert, while formal and arranged, had not been unpleasant. But this life, this little cottage by the sea with the love of all its inhabitants, their walks on the shell and stone-scattered beach, and Shane Bellows, this package of life was renewing, beyond the expectations of Anne Snow, the little girl from the lush Connecticut hills. Yes, she assured herself with a prayer of thanks, I am grateful.

Shane scrambled eggs, content with Annie sleeping longer. His entire core felt tense, thinking about her wanting to put his name on the cottage deed. What was she thinking? Was she feeling worse than she expressed? Did she think her time was limited? He took a deep breath and questioned what he would do without her in his life. From the moment he'd seen her on the beach, he'd loved her. Why, he asked his soul, did he leave her for many torturous years? Was it better to begin in a new atmosphere with new people than staying near her and not having her in his life? No.

Shane moved from the stove to the sink and looked out to the garden, his hands braced against the rim of the kitchen sink. While living in New Mexico he'd wondered hundreds of times if Annie still lived at Salt Hill and, if so, was she with another. There was never a time she was far from his thoughts, never a time when she didn't hold first place in his heart. He could not deny the truth: he should have stayed.

When Annie walked into the kitchen, a smile on her luminous face, Shane had to cough back tears in his eyes. "It's the pepper," he said, and then he moved toward her for a kiss.

Chapter Twenty-One

In quiet moments, Annie's thoughts drifted back to Connecticut, recalling her favorite brook, the meadows, the freedom she knew as a child enchanted with nature. Every time she thought of those hills and the homestead, she concluded with recalling her life in New York City. She was an eight year-old sharing a bedroom with another child dancer; traffic raging outside their window, horns blaring incessantly in early morning hours and into the dark.

Exhausted from dance routines and everyday exercises, there were no sleepless nights, but often there were dreams, always of the farm and vague figures she assumed to be her parents, her family. She thought of what she'd known and missed it all, yet there in the city was where she had been sent and applauded for her fluid moves on stage. It became evident to the child that this existence was expected of her, that no one missed her enough to reunite her with all she'd loved. When tears had threatened to emerge, she swallowed and tried to think of current choreography, how best to point her toes, which angle to position her dainty hands. Annie learned to accept what was offered, suggested, demanded.

As the gentle summer faded, the beach became more private, the town more quiet. Tourists would return at Thanksgiving, but for several sweet weeks life became serene as if in rest.

Annie steadied her life with the volunteer work at the women's shelter, finding solace and joy in teaching a few graceful steps to those hungry for more than food and clothes. Often she took beautiful scarves, gifts over the years from friends in New York, to her students, teaching them to use the fluidity of the soft material in their hands to follow as music became persuasive. Returning to the cottage after a day away, she found Shane had made sandwiches or soup and always a fresh pot of coffee. This was home.

"You know what I've been thinking?" Shane asked as they enjoyed lunch. Before Annie's smile could broaden to the question, he continued. "I think we should take this dog up north for a night or two away. What would you say to Maine, maybe the Boothbay Harbor area?"

Annie sipped coffee and met Shane's grey eyes. "I haven't ever been. It sounds intriguing."

Shane reached for her hand momentarily. "Good, then let's go. I have a project I'll finish in another two days, how's that for timing?"

Annie thought for a moment. "I think that would work. I'll go to the shelter the day after tomorrow, and then I'm yours."

Shane smiled. "You're mine all the time, don't let go of that thought."

Annie returned the smile then continued with her meal, her thoughts on how tenderly he spoke, how he was in control of them as a couple, but in an emotional, romantic manner. She remembered that when as a couple she and Albert were going to a theatre, an event of any significance, his words were a confirmation of what they were about to do – there would be no discussion. Again, Annie had been his marionette.

~

Two days later they were traveling north to Boothbay Harbor, Maine, a room arranged on the wharf area where they could enjoy walks through town with Sherlock as they listened to gulls and horns from arriving and departing boats.

As they enjoyed a meal at a water's edge restaurant, Annie watched the activities in the harbor, delighting in the colorful vessels.

"I'm so glad you chose this place to visit," Annie said. "It's absolutely wonderful."

Shane refilled her wine glass from a decanter on the table. "I thought you'd like this town."

Annie took a sip of wine and asked, "Have you been here before?"

Shane nodded. "Yes, a few months before I hit Salt Hill, I stayed here for a month. I was in search of a place to call home and I found it."

Annie cocked her head to one side. "What made you choose Salt Hill Bay?"

Shane smiled. "You."

Annie held back tears as Shane continued. "We have some great places we could explore; New England is a special area."

"Where should we go next time?"

Shane was quick to respond. "Oh, how about those Connecticut hills you hailed from?"

Annie looked out at the harbor and then back at Shane's handsome face. "Maybe."

Back at their room, they delivered to Sherlock a packet containing three broiled scallops to accompany his evening meal. A brief walk through town for the three of them was enough to lull them to sleep that night with fog horns echoing in the distance.

Back home after three days away, Annie marveled at the essence of *home*, of being where everything good in her life came together. Her first motion was to make coffee while Shane brought their suitcase inside, Sherlock following until he thumped down on the floor finding one of his favorite chew toys. His eyes followed the humans he adored. He'd been a rescue – they had *each* been a rescue.

After a warm shower and changing into a pale gray jersey pajama set, Annie sat down on the living room's sofa to brush her long, wet hair. "It's wonderful to get away," she said to Shane who sat across from her, "yet home is welcoming, secure. We're so lucky."

Shane looked at her and smiled. "Yes, we are. I can't think of a single thing I'd change about us."

It occurred to him that they didn't *need* one another as much as they *wanted* one another.

That night Annie watched as Shane sat down on the bed's edge and twisted his neck and shoulders slowly. It was obvious he had some discomfort. Without a word, she pushed the covers aside, knelt on the bed near to his back, and gently massaged the area he had begun to rub. He tilted his head to the side, enjoying the gentle hands on his body, the light kneading allowing him to relax.

She would enjoy every moment with her husband and their large dog. For the months, and hopefully years ahead, Annie would love the moments granted to them as she thought, now is what we have.

When Shane turned sideways on the bed and took her hands in his, they slipped beneath the covers, held one another, and went to sleep, Sherlock at their feet.

Close your eyes. Fall in love. Stay there.
Rumi